ACCLAIM FOR *THE PALACE THIEF* AND ETHAN CANIN

"Masterful . . . a keen and compassionate talent. His writing is cut of whole cloth; it is beautiful and it wears well."

—*New York Daily News*

"A heartening tribute to the form . . . captivating to the point that I found myself dreading the inevitable denouement. An exquisite performance."

—Gail Caldwell, *Boston Sunday Globe*

"Richly satisfying."

—*USA Today*

"Brilliant . . . Canin keeps readers so thoroughly engaged that the anticipation of resolution is almost like dread."

—*Publishers Weekly*

"Brilliantly realised and beautifully written."

—*London Times*

"*The Palace Thief* is a model of wit, wisdom, and empathy. Chekhov would have appreciated its frank renderings and quirky ironies."

—*Chicago Tribune*

"Ethan Canin's achievement is one of both artistry and humanity."
—Dan Cryer, *New York Newsday*

"This is a beautiful book, the language and structure complex but clear, every trick and turn of the writing done in the service of characters whom we can love and return to, time and again."

—*Orange County Register*

"Wonderful . . . the newest addition to what is becoming the most distinguished body of work of any young American author."

—Robert Coles

THE PALACE THIEF

THE
PALACE
THIEF

▲

ETHAN CANIN

Picador USA
New York

For information on Picador USA Reading Group Guides, as well as ordering, please contact the Trade Marketing department at St. Martin's Press.
Phone: 1-800-221-7945 extension 763
Fax: 212-677-7456
E-mail: trademarketing@stmartins.com

"Accountant" was originally published in the May 1993 issue of *Esquire* magazine. "Batorsag and Szerelem" was originally published in the July 1993 issue of *Granta* magazine. "The Palace Thief" was originally published in the Fall 1993 issue of *The Paris Review*.

ISBN 0-312-30731-4

First published in the United States by Random House, Inc.

Second Picador USA Paperback Edition: November 2002

10 9 8 7 6 5 4 3 2 1

FOR BARBARA

The author wishes to thank Po Bronson, Camille Capozzi, Chard deNiord, Alex Gansa, Dan Geller, Dayna Goldfine, Michael Goldman, Leslie Graham, Maxine Groffsky, Kate Medina, Steve Sellers, and Judith Wolff for help with this book.

THE PALACE THIEF

ACCOUNTANT
1
▲
BATORSAG AND SZERELEM
57
▲
CITY OF BROKEN HEARTS
107
▲
THE PALACE THIEF
153

I

▲

ACCOUNTANT

I am an accountant, that calling of exactitude and scruple, and my crime was small. I have worked diligently, and I do not mind saying that in the conscientious embrace of the ledger I have done well for myself over the years, yet now I must also say that due to a flaw in my character I have allowed one small trespass against my honor. I try to forget it. Although now I do little more than try to forget it, I find myself considering and reconsidering this flaw, and then this trespass, although in truth if I am to look at them both, this flaw is so large that it cannot properly be called a flaw but my character itself, and this trespass was devious. I have a wife and three children. My name is Abba Roth.

I say this as background, that is all. I make no excuses for myself, nor have I ever. The facts are as follows: We live in San Rafael, California, and I work at Priebe, Emond & Farmer, the San Francisco firm, where I have worked since the last days of the Eisenhower administration. At one time or another we have owned a Shetland pony, dug a swimming pool, leased a summer cottage at Lake Tahoe, and given generously to the Israel

General Fund, although all that we still do is lease the cottage.
My wife's name is Scheherazade, and she will not answer to
Sherri, her childhood appellation, anymore. We have two
daughters, Naomi and Rachel, and a son, whose name is Abba
also, although I know this name is not in fashion.

Recently a man I knew as a child called me at my office, and
this is how this incident began. His name is Eugene Peters and
we have known each other for most of our lives. We grew up
together in Daly City, California, a suburb of San Francisco
that, like accounting, has become the object of some scorn by
particular segments of society. A popular song has been written
on the theme that all the homes in Daly City are identical,
although this happens not to be correct. In reality there were
any number of different architectural plans used in the neighborhood where Mr. Peters and I grew up, although by coinci-
dence he and I did in fact grow up in houses that happened to
be built from the same one. The plans, of course, had been
reflected on an axis so that each house became the mirror image
of the other—each contained a living room, with the kitchen
set in a side bay, two bedrooms off a short hallway, a basement
downstairs, and on the garage side of the front yard a palm that
in our childhoods grew from a seedling to the height of the
roof. His room abutted from the left of the upstairs hall, as
mine did, in our own house, from the right; their bathroom was
on the right of the same hall and ours was on the left, et cetera,
so that it sometimes struck me as odd when the floors and walls
in his house were covered with furnishings belonging to his
parents and not my own. We rode bicycles together and later
drove in his Plymouth convertible; later still, we double-dated,
and we played on the same baseball team. I played third base
and Eugene, whose father had gone to Notre Dame with our
coach, played shortstop.

I know it is commonly assumed that a shortstop has better range than a third baseman, but in this case I can attest that such was not the case.

In those days, Eugene and I spent nearly all of our afternoons together after school. He had a sister, as did I, and his father, like mine, was never at home, so that in a funny way it might have seemed for a while that our families, in our identical houses, were interchangeable. We washed his car together. We learned to ice-skate and for a time spent our afternoons in the frosty, round rink, trying to catch the skates of girls in earmuffs who glided past us snapping their gum. We learned to roll cigarettes that burned evenly and to drink whiskey without coughing.

However, there came a time when our lives diverged. After high school I was able to benefit from the discipline my father had bestowed upon us even in his general absence and go to the state university, where I began to pursue a degree in accounting. At this point our separation became clear to us both. Mr. Peters had taken a job in an auto-parts dealership stocking inventory at the time I was learning the indifference curves and just beginning to understand where the intersection of supply and demand could be found for an inelastic commodity, such as city water. He found new friends at the auto warehouse, and I began to live my life with no friends at all. I attended school during the day, answered telephones in a hospital in the evening, and studied at night. Whenever I saw him at that time, he teased me for still living at home, although he well knew why I did.

To clarify: It became apparent that we had diverged because he was interested in the present and I was interested in the future. I do not mind saying that accounting did not come easily for me and I was studying strenuously. However, I did not waver from my commitment to it. In fact, in time I came to see that it contained a natural eloquence, unbent by human will, and that it was a more profound language than the common man might have assumed it to be. Indeed, at times I felt it was capable of explaining not only outlays and receipts but much of the natural world. It was only rarely, late at night with my books of tax law and microeconomics, that I indulged the small daydream that I might one day leave my studies and instead become a professor of music history at a small college. But I seldom indulged this thought. Indeed, I came with time to cherish my daydream for the principal reason that it challenged and therefore reinforced my resolve to make something of myself. Sitting at the window in the library, where the septate leaves of a Japanese maple brushed the glass, I would look up from Samuelson and allow my mind to wander to the third movement of Berlioz's *Requiem,* or to the second movement of Beethoven's Seventh Symphony, wherein the strings, though barely moving, weep for humankind. Then, deliberately, I would snap back to the Samuelson text and redouble the efforts that had brought me near, I do not mind saying, to the top of my class of accounting students.

Again, I say this as background. Once a week I spent the whole night awake with my books, and I took no time away except Sunday mornings, when I ate breakfast with my family, and Saturday nights, when I allowed myself a date if I could find one or a movie if I could not. Needless to say, this regimen produced a commendable record at my graduation, which Mr. Peters attended, although he did not dress correctly.

He wore a baseball cap, and I could not help noticing—I do not mind saying this with some satisfaction—that while I was graduating with honors in business accounting, my friend seemed to want nothing more than to stock gaskets and price piston rings until the short hair at his temples turned gray.

However, shortly after I graduated and had taken a job with Priebe & Emond, Mr. Peters approached me and asked for a one-thousand-dollar investment in a concern he claimed to be starting that was going to manufacture magnetic oil plugs. At the time he approached me, we hadn't spoken since my commencement exercises. He came to my office, again in a baseball cap. The idea was simple, he said: The magnetic plug would collect the flecks of metal that ordinarily circulated in the dirty oil of a car's engine and caused abrasion damage to the pistons and cylinders. Engine life would therefore be extended.

I was unsure whether any of the managing partners had seen him enter my office in a billed cap, and it goes without saying that I felt some discomfort at having him there. I was still new at the firm. To be frank, the idea seemed like a good one, but since I had just spent four years in school all day, at work all evening, and at my desk half the night while he was idling his days at a warehouse and his evenings at bars, I asked him instead whether he had ever considered the flexibility of consumer demand for his product. I asked him this instead of giving him the money. He left our offices still trying pitifully to give the impression that he had understood my question, and I went back to my job, where in six months I made my first advancement.

However, the fact is that three years later his company employed twelve men, was doing $2.3 million in gross sales and was rumored to be considering a public offering. Mr. Peters had been profiled in the business section of the newspaper, and in that photograph he wore the same baseball cap he had worn at my commencement and in my office. Indeed, the cap seemed to have become a sort of a symbol for him, although I do not know of what. The magnetic oil plugs had been picked up by at least two major auto-parts chains, and I saw them for sale everywhere I went. I changed the supermarket where I shopped because one day I found the oil plugs for sale there. My friend's company had also begun manufacturing an auto emergency kit that sold well to women and accounted for a good deal of his profits. He was diversifying. Though we didn't speak anymore, I saw him driving a blue Chrysler New Yorker and heard through our old friends that he had bought a sixteen-room house in Hillsborough and a villa with boat bays at Lake Tahoe. By now several of our high school classmates worked for him.

I myself was not making a bad salary at the time. In fact, I was doing quite well, and I do not mind saying that if not for the success of my friend I would have considered myself perfectly fortunate in my business advancement. Mr. Emond, the elder partner at my firm, had taken an interest in me, and by working late and servicing extra accounts I had elicited a promise from him that I would be made partner within five years.

At this point I decided to marry. At the time I was seeing two girls, LeAnne and Scheherazade. LeAnne was the assistant in the office of my dentist, and one morning while she was placing the light-blue paper bib around my neck for a teeth cleaning, I asked her outright to have dinner with me. I fell in love with her immediately. On one of our early evenings together at a moderately expensive Greek restaurant a man at the next table suffered a coronary, and without hesitation LeAnne moved aside the furniture and laid him down, keeping her hand on his pulse until the ambulance arrived. That kind of levelheadedness attracted me. On another occasion a skirt she had purchased at a department store ripped along a seam and LeAnne took it back there, where she had to speak not just with a sales clerk but with the manager of the entire operation. Though he tried to intimidate her, saying she had purchased it on sale, LeAnne persisted and gained the return of her money. I don't mind saying that this kind of respect for the value of a dollar won my heart as well.

At the same time I was seeing Scheherazade. In my situation I felt that I needed some objectivity, and this was what Scheherazade became for me. As I found myself falling further in love with LeAnne, I went on more dates with Scheherazade. During the course of one evening with her we came upon the scene of an auto accident, and instead of getting out to help as LeAnne might have done, Scheherazade pressed me to drive on and nearly fainted from the sight as we passed. I became more convinced of my love for LeAnne. Furthermore, when we dined out Scheherazade ordered smoked-salmon appetizers and baked desserts that she left mostly untouched on her plate. Of course I had enough money to pay for the whole menu had she chosen to order it, but still, this represented a certain difference between her and LeAnne.

In fact there was only one incident that made me consider Scheherazade more seriously. As I did with LeAnne as well, Scheherazade and I occasionally went to the symphony. At the concerts I was always proud to be seen with LeAnne, for she wore elegant though simple dresses and spoke with a level eye to whomever we met. Scheherazade sometimes came in sleeveless gowns and heels that had been embedded with glitter, her lips made up in sienna-colored lipstick and her hair tossed over her head and stuck with a pearl-headed stickpin. In general I preferred going with LeAnne. As I have said, my small dream was to become a professor of music, and it was not insignificant that LeAnne always read the back-notes to the program. She always knew something of the composer's life for our discussions after the concerts, whereas Scheherazade, who often appeared to be dreaming during the performance, often did not even know who had written the evening's music.

One night, however, during an intermission after we had heard Berlioz's *Romeo and Juliet*, Scheherazade waited on the open-air balcony while I purchased soft drinks for us at the bar.

When I came out, I found her leaning against the railing, and in the lights of the city square below I could see that she was weeping. Full streams of tears were on her cheeks. I asked her what was wrong, and she only shook her head. I tried to think about what might have occurred in her life. As I stood there with the two soft drinks I asked her if her mother's health was still good. I asked if there had been an embarrassment at work or with one of her friends. I asked her about her brother, who had recently moved to New York. I asked her if she needed money. Finally I left her alone. I moved to the balcony rail and reviewed some pension documentation that I had been working on that morning. Suddenly it occurred to me that she was crying over the music. I am not embarrassed to say that this touched a part of me quite deeply, and I felt grateful to have finally understood. I myself have never cried at anything, not at a movie nor at a play nor at a concert, and I don't see why it should have pleased me that Scheherazade had. But it did. It was a small thing, but I didn't think LeAnne would have done it.

In the spring after I was promised the partnership in my firm I decided to ask LeAnne to marry me. I placed a deposit hold on a one-and-a-half-carat diamond ring and began to plan my proposal. The days were growing longer, and often in the evenings we took walks in the pale green hills south of San Francisco. Behind me on those paths the determined sound of her breaths filled me with the sense that the future was ours. A culmination was building, and one evening in those hills I realized that such would be the place to propose. The next night we walked up a new trail, and in the distance I saw a small, level plot of ground that looked out over all of San Francisco Bay and the foothills across it to the east. I pretended to twist my ankle and prevailed on LeAnne to turn around before she saw the vista, but I decided that at this spot in two weeks' time I would ask her to be my bride.

However, as soon as I made this decision I began to see her in another light. Suddenly her practical nature became a sort of shrewishness. Her steady demeanor became a source of irritation and an indication that in certain situations she might become unbending. By this point I had added to my holding deposit on the ring and was well along toward its purchase. Sometimes I looked at LeAnne and it was as if a demon had taken hold of my soul. I saw her pettiness and the unchangeable tenacity of her perceptions. I began to regard her thriftiness as penury and her practical nature as mannish. One night at a concert she remarked that ticket prices were certainly going to increase next season, and suddenly I found myself thinking back to the night Scheherazade had wept on the balcony.

Now, I have always considered myself a practical man. That is what an accountant is paid for. He is not paid to encourage foundless business schemes nor to weep at public concerts. When an accountant considers a decision, he extrapolates to outcomes and weighs the assets and liabilities. However, two weeks later, when I made the final payment on the ring, I found myself offering it to Scheherazade and not to LeAnne, and seven months later in the ballroom at the Clift Hotel, Scheherazade and I were dancing at our wedding.

I must add that our marriage has now lasted nearly three decades, and even as our passion has subsided it has been replaced by a spring of tenderness and gratitude at which I drink now as reverently as a pilgrim. I have never said this before, however, and I do not like to say it now, but I must also add that on the day of our wedding I felt gloomy. When the rabbi signaled past the congregation for my bride to approach, my heart leapt in panic, and when he gestured to the cantor at the blessing, I felt doomed. This was a secret I carried forth into the twenty-nine years of our life together. During this time, by the way, I have divined through careful conversation that a similar feeling was present in the hearts of several of my fellow accountants during their own nuptials.

It has not escaped my attention that perhaps Scheherazade sensed my gloom and it was for this reason that she began spending my money like a bandit. In one year, unable to settle on a pattern for our living room drapes, she installed three separate sets. Our living room, I should add, is large, and so are its windows. Of course, I could afford ten sets of drapes, but that is not the point.

I did not mention the money to her because it was my duty to provide and that is what I was doing. In fact I spent little for myself. This as everyone knows is a value instilled in childhood, and I have my own mother to thank for it. When the soles of my shoes wore through I repaired them with vinyl glue, as my mother used to do with my father's, and when my barber began charging sophisticated rates for his haircuts I went elsewhere. However, though I had intended to reduce our monthly expenditures by such practices, I soon understood that I would not be able to.

It was as though the more I tried to economize, the more she tried to waste. I began servicing extra accounts during my lunch hour, while at auction one day Scheherazade purchased a small etching by Goya, in front of which I found her standing when I returned home from the office. It was only a few inches tall, depicting a farmhouse and several chickens, yet she had placed it in the center of our living room wall. Over the course of months I saw that she was capable of standing before it for a half hour at a stretch, and I must concede that at times like this I felt no closer to understanding my wife than I would have been to a pygmy. The following year she purchased a terra-cotta figurine from the Han Dynasty, smaller than my thumb, which she set on our mantle and which now and then I found her holding in her hands, late at night, when I ventured downstairs for seltzer water.

Nonetheless, I soon grew accustomed to our charge-account balances, and in the decade before our children were born we reached an equilibrium in our marriage. Indeed, these were the first times in which I can say that I was blissfully content. Thursday evenings at the symphony we stood outdoors on the octagonal balcony at intermission, and while Scheherazade gazed dreamily over the square I pursued in my mind some of the tax shelters and bankruptcy manipulations that had become a standard part of my practice. Such evenings were the embodiment of happiness for me. I felt I was about to be made a partner and had again heard news to that effect from Mr. Emond. My salary was as high as I had ever hoped to earn, and with stock options I could look forward to being a reasonably wealthy man in a decade.

Mr. Peters, however, had in the meantime expanded his auto-parts business into four factories in three states and had opened a chain of retail outlets. Furthermore, he had for some reason seized on the idea of baseball as a theme for his advertisements, which began to appear in the newspaper. I do not see what the connection is between automobile parts and our national pastime, but a smiling portrait of Eugene Peters wearing his baseball cap began to appear in the corner of these announcements, accompanied by slogans like "Doubleheader Sale" or "All-Star Prices." One evening, watching the seven-o'clock news, I was startled to see that he had begun purchasing television commercials as well, and that he himself narrated them. Again, he wore the baseball cap. Needless to add, I soon found his ads on my car radio as well when I drove to work in the morning, although I cannot say with certainty whether he was the narrator of these. It does not take a professional psychologist to observe that he was probably attempting to compensate for his two seasons of high school play, which were stellar neither at bat nor in the field. Within a short space of time a number of retired professional players began making cameo appearances at the end of these ads. These were minor players such as the back-up catcher for the World Championship 1954 Giants and a utility infielder from the team of 1962, and I will not bother with their names. However, I suppose it meant he was hobnobbing with these retired athletes, and although I do not know why, this thought irritated me. I had no desire to know of his successes, yet I found myself reading certain items in the business pages. The thousand dollars he had once asked me for might well have been a small fortune by now, and I myself might have been hobnobbing with these players, but by a simple act of will I was able to put this from my mind.

At home Scheherazade became pregnant with Naomi. I will remember the day I learned I was to become a father because my wife called me at work, which she rarely did, and because when I came home that day I found that she had purchased for herself an ermine stole. I do not mind saying that the sight of the ermine hanging in our closet when I went to hang up my own raincoat was more than I ordinarily would have tolerated, but given Scheherazade's announcement, I felt in no position to object. In June Naomi was born.

It was at about this time that Mr. Peters entered our lives again. We received a letter inviting us to dinner, and I accepted, although the letter had been written by his secretary. I had Naomi's college education to plan for now and was ready to consider and yet remain prudent about any business offer he might make. Naomi's money was in government bonds. Sensing that he would be asking me for another investment, I carefully calculated what I could afford to risk on a venture such as his. I arrived at a sum that, I do not mind saying, would surely have pleased him.

Scheherazade and I met Mr. Peters at the Squire Room Restaurant in the Fairmont Hotel, where we ate an elaborate dinner including a bottle of burgundy dating from the Second World War and a bottle of port dating from the First. Although needless to say I would not have ordered these vintages myself, I nonetheless attempted to pay for them at the end of the meal. Mr. Peters, however, had evidently made a prior arrangement with the waiter. I have gone over in my mind several times what occurred that evening. I had a reasonably pleasant time and I think he did, too. However, at the end of our meal, Scheherazade without hesitation ordered two different desserts, eating only part of one of them and leaving the other untouched. Mr. Peters did not seem to mind, and he even joked about it. However, he made no business offers.

In short succession Rachel and Abba were born. I had not yet been made partner at the firm because the position of Mr. Emond had been temporarily weakened, yet my own standing was still strong and I was earning in two months what my father used to earn in a year. I had developed a technique that was quite successful in recruiting new clients. I would take them to a meal at a nearby restaurant that had arrangements with the firm, where I would talk about professional sports or, if I could discern a leaning, the current political situation. I would not mention any business proposal until the table had been cleared. At this point, the maitre d' would approach, recognize me by name, and offer us an aperitif "as his guest." This, as I said, was by arrangement, and though I always asked for Grand Marnier,

I was brought scotch whiskey in an apertif glass instead, which I would then drain in a single draft. The whiskey could be counted on in the course of seconds to bring about a temporary, garrulous ease that I exploited by leaning toward the potential client and saying, in an offhand way that came easily after the cocktail, "Say, I bet they sock you at tax time."

Every partner at the firm had such a method, in one form or another, that produced results, and over the experience of numerous years I found that my particular entreaty worked quite well with the genre of client with whom I had most contact, specifically attorneys, physicians, and the not-infrequent movie or television actor—members of the professions, in other words, that required a certain ease with the public. Of course, I could vary my approach. Meeting, as we sometimes did, with the financial staff of corporations, I certainly would not try the "socked at tax time" approach. In those situations, of course, Mr. Priebe or Mr. Emond was present alongside, and the entreaty was a formal one, made in advance of the meeting, carefully considered against competing bids and factually represented in documents.

In summary, I was able to do well at the firm, where I earned a good salary and good bonuses and was well on my way to a partnership, although I suppose I should mention another incident that occurred several years ago. At the time the firm still went by the name Priebe & Emond, as Paul Farmer had not yet been made a principal. One morning, before most of the other accountants and any of the secretaries were at their desks, Mr. Priebe appeared in my doorway and asked in a low voice whether I was free to see him in his office. There, we sat in the two padded chairs next to his window, which looked out over the Bay Bridge to the north and the shipyards to the east. Noticing that I was interested in the view, he chatted for several minutes about the enormous tonnage of concrete contained within the bridge's bulwarks; then he abruptly turned to the wall and asked me if I knew anything of what had been recently occurring in the savings and loan industry. Being familiar with the trade journals, I replied that I knew something of what was occurring then. It is important to note that this meeting between Mr. Priebe and myself occurred at least two years before the savings and loan affair became known to the public. Mr. Priebe then looked me in the eye and asked me what I would think of an accountant who knowingly doctored books to protect the partners in a government-backed savings institution. I understood that I was under consideration for a partnership at the firm and knew immediately that this was a test of my moral principles. "I would not approve," I responded.

"I didn't think you would," said Mr. Priebe, nodding, and then he rose to shake my hand, signaling that our meeting was over. Two days later, Mr. Emond entered my office during the lunch hour and told me that he had heard what had happened and was proud of my response. I myself was as well, of course, and I continued my regular duties with increasing expectation of a promotion. However, within a month it was Mr. Farmer who received the partnership.

It is fruitless for me to speculate about what occurred, although I did notice that prior to his promotion Mr. Farmer had become more secretive about his work and was now often already in the office when I arrived in the morning. That is all I will say about this matter.

Without omitting anything of importance, I have skipped to the year when Naomi was fifteen, Rachel thirteen, and Abba nine. To my astonishment the children had grown up each with a distinct personality. Naomi was dark in all her features, in her hair and skin and the cast of her eyes, and dark in her character

as well. In our garden she sat in the plum tree's deep shade, and
at the table she ate without speaking. She had found a natural
kinship with my wife that at times pleased me, for Naomi was
my favorite, but I must say that at other times I felt the two of
them were in collusion against me. They often went shopping
together and sometimes returned with several twine-handled
bags that they refused to open for me, laughing darkly to each
other while they brought them upstairs to the bedrooms. At
home Naomi often sat by herself. The brooding postures she
assumed and the reticence with which she expressed her affec-
tions made her occasional demonstrations of love exquisite
morsels that I pined for. Sometimes while I worked at my desk
upstairs she would enter my study, walk up behind me and
without saying anything place a hand on each of my shoulders.
If I spoke, she withdrew them, so that often I did my work
silently, scrutinizing the account books of physicians and attorneys while in the corner of my vision the dark fingers of my
daughter lay unmoving. We hardly ever spoke. I believe she
knew she was my favorite, and for a reason I do not understand,
this excited in her a sense of injustice. Her tastes, like my wife's,
were extravagant.

Rachel, on the other hand, was everything Naomi was not.
She had blond hair and pale, warm skin that rushed to color
when she was excited, which was often. Where Naomi at the
age of thirteen had worn small pearl earrings, Rachel wore boys'
sneakers and dressed in the same dungarees for a week. Rachel
sat in the open, sunlit portion of our yard and practiced her field
hockey in our living room. When I returned from work, she
hugged me around the legs and begged for a ride on my feet,
which I more often than not gave her, holding her by her pale
arms and lifting her small sneakers across the Afghani carpet
atop my oxfords, which I did not mind shining again later. On

Sundays Rachel dusted the windowsills without asking and emptied the small inlaid wastebasket in my study. I often found my pencils sharpened and the clips and erasers arranged in rows in my desk, and I made sure to thank Rachel whenever this occurred. Rachel, I believe, knew that Naomi was my favorite, though it is odd that in Naomi this situation produced forlornness and brooding, while in Rachel it created only exuberance.

As for Abba, he was a son and his childhood passed without the trouble and wondering I had found with my daughters. I bought him baseball gloves and football cleats and felt certain this was enough to pass him forward through his boyhood. He had an even disposition. He spoke softly and in general took easily to the world. He had no problems with his friends nor with his teachers, and he seemed to have missed his sister's propensity to spend my money. Indeed, if it were not for Scheherazade's intervention, I believe he might never have bought a thing for himself.

As I said, this was not true for my elder daughter. When Naomi was sixteen, for example, she decided she wanted a horse. Her high school had offered an equestrian course, and against my wishes she had learned to ride. One night soon after, she brought up the idea of owning a horse, and in response I could not help snorting, much like a horse myself. My own father was a wristwatch salesman, and I told Naomi that the descendants of such people did not own horses. Some of them *shoed* horses, I said, but none owned them. Naomi furrowed her dark brow. I thought the matter was ended, but several days later Scheherazade turned over in bed and mentioned that Naomi was at a brooding age and perhaps I ought to consider her request.

We bought the horse from a young man who lived in a mansion in Woodside. He wore riding britches that looked as if they had been ordered from a men's catalogue, and when I gave him my check he asked to see my driver's license. Naomi mounted the beast, and as she sat there it stamped its hooves and flared its agate-colored nostrils. "Thank you, Daddy," she said as she turned and started around the show ring.

The animal had cost as much as an automobile, and as she paraded it around the ring, her back arched, her high boots pressed into its flanks, I quickly calculated the feed and stable costs on a per-year basis. We had it boarded in a private stable. Like Naomi, the animal turned out to have a dark temperament, and like Naomi's, this temperament was most prominent in regard to its benefactor. Naomi named him Dreamboat, which I did not like. I did not believe that a horse could differentiate among human beings; whenever I approached, however, Dreamboat flared his nostrils and snorted, and whenever I spoke he stamped his hooves. The thought occurred to me that he knew who had written the check for his purchase. On the other hand, whenever Naomi or Rachel or Scheherazade spoke to him, he flicked his tail and bowed his protuberant head, and whenever they approached with oats, he blinked his eyes like a lover. Abba, for his part, took after me and did not seem to notice the beast. For several months Naomi rode every day, and then she began riding a few times per week, and soon after that she stopped riding altogether. Dreamboat developed an infection in his leg. Antibiotics were needed, and when these failed, a veterinary surgeon. Up until that time I had thought there were no professionals more expensive than a physician. Dreamboat never recovered, and a year later he was taken from his agony.

I shall not mention other examples of the spendthriftery that was a disease in my house. As I have said previously, at one time or another we have dug a pool in our backyard, leased a cottage near the beach at Lake Tahoe, and given to a number of my wife's charities. All the while I had three children in private schools and was afflicted with the standard concerns of any father. Scheherazade had never worked, and I needed to think of her security should something happen to me. And after private high school, of course, our children would expect private college.

Therefore, it was with careful consideration that I reacted when, shortly over one month ago, I again had contact with Eugene Peters. I was working at my desk at Priebe, Emond & Farmer when Mrs. Polaris, my secretary, came on the speaker phone to inform me that Mr. Peters was on the line. Naturally this was a surprise, he and I not having spoken in several years, since the evening of our fruitless dinner at the Fairmont Hotel. I organized the papers I was studying, a rather complicated profit-and-loss statement from a sophisticated client, closed the volumes of tax code that were on my desk, replaced them in their alphabetical slots on my shelves, returned to my chair, leaned back in it, and answered the call. However, it was not Mr. Peters but his secretary on the line. "Please hold for Mr. Peters," she said.

The line went quiet and I rang Mrs. Polaris again and asked her to wait on the line for Mr. Peters; then I sat back again in my chair and, resting my eyes on the speaker telephone in front of me, pleasantly noted the cool breeze that was at that moment entering through my window. Finally, after a pause, the telephone chimed, indicating a call transfer, and Mrs. Polaris passed Mr. Peters on to me. "Eugene," I said, picking up the phone, "I'm sorry to make you wait."

"I have a proposition," he said.

I do not need to explain that in the business world one proposition is often nothing more than the camouflage for another, and as I sat back in my chair noting the details of what he proposed, a pattern took form in my mind. He had called to tell me something rather ridiculous, that he and a group of fellows had arranged to spend a week that January in Scottsdale, Arizona, at a San Francisco Giants fantasy camp. I knew about these fantasy camps from an article in *The Wall Street Journal*, but I asked him questions anyway, because there are times in business when one ought to act as though one is uninformed, and I was well aware that this call was business. I let him tell me that the fantasy camp was an opportunity for athletic men such as ourselves to play live baseball against some of the Giants' stars of the past era, such as Tito Fuentes, Dick Dietz, and Ken Henderson. The food was first-class, Mr. Peters went on, the accommodations were excellent, and business seminars were held in the evenings. One of the fellows had become otherwise engaged, Mr. Peters told me, and the long and the short of it was that a position was now open. Did I want to fill it? He mentioned the cost, close to four thousand dollars for the week, and I assured him that this was not what mattered to me. I was quick to laugh at this, and told him I would call him in the afternoon after Mrs. Polaris had a moment to consult my schedule.

I hung up and sat thinking. It is phrases like this "group of fellows" that one must be on the lookout for in business, for such a group of fellows can in fact turn out to be a set of industry leaders, chairmen of the board, or senators. It is not like going to the bowling alley with a "group of guys." In fact, what had taken shape in my mind as Mr. Peters and I exchanged jovial barbs about his old inability to hit the curveball and my own occasionally erratic throw to first—although, for the record, my throw is quite reliable—was that in fact he was hoping to use the opportunity at baseball camp to offer me a business proposal.

I don't mind saying that I became a bit agitated. I went out into the anteroom of my office and stood behind Mrs. Polaris's desk, looking out the window and reviewing the near misses Mr. Peters and I had had in our dealings. I obviously had made the correct decision the first time he had approached me, for in those days he was an uneducated man with neither the sense nor the appearance for business, and he had not in any reasonable view made analysis of the market. That he succeeded with his venture, indeed, was luck. The second time, he had of course something of a record in the marketplace, and I will not conceal the fact that I was disposed to invest; yet something occurred in our exchange at the Fairmont Hotel that precluded an offer. Although I do not know exactly what it was, I now see the possibility that it was an error to have brought along my wife. It is of no use to think like this, however.

In any case, at Mrs. Polaris's window now, it seemed perfectly possible that another opportunity was at hand: To wit, I suspected that Mr. Peters was going to approach me at this fantasy camp with another bid for investment. I quickly reviewed in my head my own portfolio, which I had weighted toward bonds in light of the unstable stock market and toward shorter maturities in light of the uncertain future. It seemed once again, I am happy to say, that I could make him a pleasing offer.

And then, of course, I suddenly understood that Mr. Peters had no need for my money. I don't mind saying that I had over the years taken enough interest in his businesses to know that he was heavily capitalized, unencumbered with debt service, and clearly poised for expansion, yet it did not occur to me until that moment, standing at Mrs. Polaris's window, that he wanted me for another reason. Business, of course, is both science and intuition, and this was a moment of intuition.

Mrs. Polaris was typing, and I moved behind her. Because of

an architectural quirk, the view from her window runs unob-
structed to San Francisco Bay, whereas my own is temporarily
obstructed by the back of a newly built hotel. (Obviously, the
hotel is not temporary; however, I will be in another office
soon.) This hotel has caused quite a stir in this city for its
architectural ingenuity, although it can be safely said that any
ingenuity is strictly confined to the front quarters of the building; my own view, in back, is limited to the ventilation shafts,
to the rows of rather shabby casement windows, already dripping rust stains at their corners, and to the constant flow of beer
salesmen hefting their kegs, florists picking among their buckets
of blooms, health inspectors in cheap suits, trash collectors with
their hats on backward, and butchers, who on Friday mornings
converge on the banquet kitchen carrying pig carcasses over
their shoulders like duffel bags.

"Have I neglected something, Mr. Roth?" said Mrs. Polaris.

"Not at all, Ina," I responded.

The fact is that I prefer my own view, full as it is of the
suggestive hubbub of commerce, to that of Mrs. Polaris, which
is so placid and beautiful that it suggests to me the shame of
failed ambition; but to contemplate a question one needs an
uninterrupted vista, and that is why I stood at the window of
my secretary. Whitecaps were chalking the bay.

"Ina," I said, "would you believe that a grown man would
pay close to four thousand to spend a week with a few baseball
players from his childhood?"

"Yes, I would," she said, resuming her typing.

I regarded her. Mrs. Polaris is a matronly woman with neat
white hair, plainly coiffed, who gives the distinct impression of
having been betrayed. I do not know if this has been by a
husband, or by her children, or by another relation I have not
imagined, yet in her presence I cannot help thinking that it has

been by me. It is not that she says anything about it, for she does not; it is merely a sense I receive from her.

"To me," I said, "It's ridiculous and a foolish waste of money. If you want to play baseball, go to the park and play. If you want to see professional baseball players, attend a professional game. It's as ridiculous for me to want to play baseball with Tito Fuentes as it would be for Tito Fuentes to come in here to prepare his own Schedule Nines."

I had tried not to permit my voice to rise, but I am afraid it had. Mrs. Polaris kept typing. I again had the impression that I had overacted around her, that she had in some way come to expect a rise in my voice or an unpleasant stridor in my bearing. As I have said, however, there is no basis for such a feeling on her part. In the corner of the picture window a luxury liner had come into view, steaming for the Golden Gate, and when the whole ship had appeared, traversed Mrs. Polaris's segment of window, and disappeared again behind the jamb, I walked around the desk and stood in front of her. I proceeded to address her in a lower voice.

"Could you imagine that?" I said, chuckling, "Tito Fuentes coming in to prepare his own Schedule Nines?"

"No, I couldn't," she said.

"Ridiculous."

Mrs. Polaris rose from her desk, went to the window and adjusted the blinds, and as she did so my thoughts turned suddenly to the fact that if I did not spend the four thousand dollars on baseball for myself, Scheherazade would spend it on Persian carpets.

"However," I said, "there may be an important business reason for me to attend the camp."

I stood in front of her, a slight smile on my lips, and although I would have preferred her to ask me what that business reason was—for I am not so successful that I cannot feel pleasure from relating my business victories to a willing ear—she did not ask me anything, and in fact took her seat again and resumed typing. I went back to my own office. It was a Friday, so I looked into the alley and waited for the butcher trucks to arrive.

That evening when I arrived home, Scheherazade and Naomi were playing backgammon together in our sunroom, on an ivory board that I had never seen before. "Where did that board come from?" I inquired. "And what do the elephants think?"

"What does the gorilla think?" said Naomi, which caused both of them to giggle darkly.

"Well," I said, "you'll never guess who called me today."

Naomi was wearing a portable radio on her belt, which I had not noticed until she reached to her ears now and shifted the speakers.

"You won't believe who called me today."

"Who?" said my wife.

"You'll never guess."

Naomi threw the dice and made her move, and my wife leaned over the board.

"It was Eugene Peters," I said.

Scheherazade looked up. I have not mentioned before that my wife is a beautiful woman who has become only more beautiful as I have known her. Her bone structure is Scandinavian, and although this might imply a harshness to her features, her beauty is softened by the gentle look of her eyes, which appear always to be misted.

"He wants me to go on a vacation with him," I said.

"Oh?"

"Although I had an insight about the business reason that may be involved."

"I wouldn't go," she said.

"I believe I realized why he wants me to come along."

"He's trying to humiliate you."

"Pardon."

"He's trying to humiliate you, and you don't even see it."

"That's ridiculous."

"Remember what happened last time."

At this point I moved back into the kitchen, where I sat down at the table, turned on the radio, and poured myself a glass of cranberry juice. I should explain what my wife was referring to. She believes that our dinner with Eugene Peters at the Fairmont Hotel was in fact some sort of play on Mr. Peters's part intended to denigrate me in regard to our relative standings in the business world. Needless to say, I have pointed out that this sort of dinner is commonplace in business and can signify any number of intentions, from an entreaty to a reconnaissance to a friendly repast, and that no denigration was intended. She, however, has insisted in the course of several conversations that Eugene Peters was "pulling my chain." Needless to say, I have assured Scheherazade that he was not, although I have not mentioned to her my own theory, which as I have said, involves desserts.

As Scheherazade had made no move to come in from her game of backgammon, I finished my cranberry juice and went upstairs to find Rachel. She was in her bedroom braiding her hair, and when I entered she came across and hugged me. "Peanut," I said, "you'll never guess who called me today."

"Mr. Peters," she answered immediately. She sat at her vanity and faced me. "I heard you out the window," she said. "What did he want?"

"He wants me to go on vacation with him, and I figured out why."

"Why, Daddy?"

"He doesn't want another investment. He's too well capitalized for that. What he wants—" I said. I folded my hands. "What he wants is for our firm to take over his accounting."

It is difficult to describe the pleasure I felt in those first few hours after we had disembarked from the airplane at Tucson and been chauffeured in by van to our accommodations at the fantasy camp. Our rooms were private and luxurious and their windows looked out over the groomed playing fields to which we would be fanning out in the morning. The hiss and rat-tat of sprinklers filled the air. Not only were we about to play the game whose dearness to my heart I clearly and immediately recalled from my childhood, but I also felt the sudden, heady pleasure of having won the professional respect of Mr. Peters. He was a wealthy and influential man and it was obvious that he planned to ask me for my services. It is one of the pleasures of life that conscientious study and diligent labor are rewarded in the end.

Swallows darted above the dark fields. On the coffee table sat a vase of fresh flowers and on the nightstand a plate of chocolates. Opening the closet door I found my uniform. It hung from a hanger within a plastic dry-cleaner's bag and I will describe it. The piping was orange, the number was sewn both on the back and on the shoulders (mine was 59, which I was not able to identify with any stars of the past), and the carefully scripted Giants emblem arced gently in the traditional manner, so that it would appear level when the uniform was donned. The black stirrup leggings buckled into the knickers, the belt was stitched into the waistband, and the pants contained the classic single pocket, at the left hip, for the hat. I donned the entire uniform immediately, a fact I am not embarrassed to admit because I know that anyone who has ever worn one will understand the sentimental reasons for doing so, although of course we would not be playing until the morning. Indeed I considered taking a stroll out to the fields at that very moment, for I could smell the new mowings and suddenly felt the childhood urge to ball them in my fingers. However, I assumed that the other men were looking out from their own windows as well, and I decided to stay in. I doffed my uniform and slept soundly.

By daybreak the sprinklers had stopped and from my room the fields appeared strewn with diamonds. I sat on the sill and contemplated the state of the world, as one often does in such situations. How could I have known that our economy would enter a prolonged and deep recession and that profits at our own firm, which had been robust, would undergo a correction? It stood to reason that Mr. Emond, as the eldest of the principals, would again be weakened in this new footing and that my own advancement might once again be delayed. Profits at Mr. Peters's firm, on the other hand, had remained stable, as his products were low-cost items such as the magnetic oil plug, which in fact reduced the necessity of future high-cost procedures such as oil changes. The fact was, I realized as I gazed over the glistening fields, that he was well positioned and we were not.

I went to my briefcase and removed the documents I had brought, detailed explanations of our services and fees in regard to high-inventory, multiple-point-of-sale businesses such as Mr. Peters's, including several innovations that I am proud of but cannot discuss. Of course these had been reviewed and approved by Mr. Farmer and Mr. Priebe, whose signatures stood below mine on the penultimate page of the proposal. The entire document had been bound in the imprinted leather portfolio cover that the firm reserved for its more important clients, and I will admit that I felt a certain pride to be carrying it. To wit, I had never made such a large proposal without one of our principals alongside.

Presently the groundskeepers appeared, two Mexican men in white trousers, and my thoughts returned to baseball. They raked the infield briskly, set the bases on their spikes, and then turned their attentions to a section of the right-field fence, which apparently had come loose at an earlier time. As they unscrewed this section and lifted it from its housing, I was pleasantly reminded of the old days of major league play, when groundskeepers moved the fences in or out depending on the batting strength of the visiting team. It appeared to me that, despite advances in the state of our society, something had been lost in the ensuing years. With a start I realized I was late for breakfast.

Returning to the task at hand, I decided after brief thought to wear my uniform to the dining area because it seemed to me that most of the other men would do so as well. Thus I donned it, shaved quickly, and went downstairs, where I found breakfast under way. Indeed I had chosen correctly concerning the uniform, as I now gazed out on the two long tables filled with men similarly dressed. One table wore the home colors and the other the traveling.

My own uniform was home colors, and I was relieved to scan the table and see that Mr. Peters's was as well. One of the men gestured to me, and I took the place next to him. The man introduced himself as Randall Forbes, shook my hand forcefully, and mentioned that he too was a friend of Mr. Peters, who now sat across from us. An older man, who I would later discover had been the batting coach for the Cleveland Indians two decades ago, came out from the kitchen and set down in front of me a plate heaping with waffles. I noticed that most of the men were not speaking, so I gestured in a friendly way to Mr. Peters and Mr. Forbes, then rubbed my hands together in pantomime of hunger and began eating my breakfast.

However, it was not long before I realized the cause for the near silence in the dining area. In fact, only one conversation was taking place, a low affair at our end of the table two seats away from me, and it was not until I had eaten one of the waffles and cut up the second that I glanced over and saw that one of those conversing was none other than Willie Mays.

How can I describe what it was like to eat a Belgian waffle with such a man sitting nearby? Of course I had expected players like a Dick Dietz or a Tito Fuentes, but now two chairs away from me sat the greatest player of his era and one of the great players of all time. Immediately my throat constricted and my mouth became dry. I believe I finished the waffles in front of me, although I have no memory of doing so. I soon understood that they were talking about the elbow difficulties of the current 49ers quarterback, and I will say that Willie Mays talking about football was enough to make me chuckle. Of course, why should he not talk about it? Indeed, although it seemed ironic to me, none of the other men returned the small smile I made looking up from my plate.

I shall take a moment to describe Mr. Mays. His hair had begun to gray, and although his face had broadened—there seemed to be a sort of general thickening to his features that spoke perhaps of his recent misfortunes concerning major league baseball—he nonetheless moved and spoke with a yawning, feline expansiveness that suggested great strength in reserve. Although he was merely eating a waffle, I can say that his limbs moved like clockwork. That is to say, as though they were attached within him to gears that moved independently. He possessed the unmistakable aura of greatness. I believe that all of us in one way or another were watching his small movements—the way he braced his knife against the inside of his wrist before cutting his waffle or the manner in which he gripped his glass of orange juice at the rim—and every one of these gestures possessed the clarity of motion one might expect in a juggler, an acrobat, or a magician. Among the men, only Eugene Peters was at ease.

Immediately after breakfast we took to the fields for warm-ups, which began with the group of us running two laps around the entire complex of four baseball diamonds facing one another. Each had dugouts, an overhanging backstop, several rows of bleachers, and the low, curved, asymmetric fence around the outfield. One of the diamonds was surrounded by a larger fan area, fifty or sixty rows of bleachers stretching in a semicircle up to the white Arizona sky, and as we jogged past these seats it seemed to me that we could have been professional players jogging to our positions. I will admit, however, that by the time Mr. Peters and I crossed the last flag in left field and jogged toward home, our breath pounding and our feet lumbering on the grass, I was seized with the idea that I had wasted my money on a foolish dream.

The whole week's endeavor had cost thirty-four hundred dollars in advance, not inclusive of bats, which we brought along ourselves. I personally had purchased three, because although each one was "indestructible," I remembered that depending on the humidity and temperature and the limberness of my arms, I sometimes preferred a heavier bat or one with a more narrow taper. In the style of our current era they were anodized aluminum instead of wood, and of course they were rubberized at the handle rather than taped. Although the money was not important to me, I will note that they cost forty-five dollars each.

Other men were gathering at the dugout. These men were financial officers, physicians, and attorneys. One stood peering out from the steps with his foot on top of the low wall, the way I remembered my own heroes used to stand—the Alou brothers, Mickey Mantle, Willie Mays himself—although this man probably worked in an office and would be sleeping with a heating pad tonight like the rest of us.

We threw that first day, fielded ground balls, and hit against the old man who ran the camp, a fellow named Corsetti who had pitched two seasons thirty years ago. He was older than we were. I guessed he was almost sixty, and he pitched with the old man's limited, eccentric motion on the mound. He had no leg kick. The arms came together in the glove at chest height, and then the ball was on its way. My first at-bat it came faster than I thought, and I swung like a man trying to catch a bird in his bare hands. "Don't hurt yourself," the catcher said through his mask. The old man on the mound threw a curveball next, and I fell back out of the box. I heard the catcher snort. But the next pitch I hit on a line into center field. I shall never forget the pop of the bat in my hands. However, I am not too vain to say that after my previous swing I had seen the catcher make a sign with his glove, and I believe the pitch I hit might have been lobbed.

In summary, our first day was uneventful, although it is of human interest to note how quickly one can become used to the presence of Willie Mays. The first time I tossed a ball to him in the warm-up throws, my arm quaked in nervousness, but my throw was a good one and I had no reason to be embarrassed by it. Willie Mays caught it without comment and sent it on to the next player. I suppose the camp needed to be concerned with injuries, and therefore on the first day we ran infield and outfield drills and each man took a turn in the box, but we did not begin actual play.

That night we heard a lecture on the current tax laws. In case anything of value was said I brought my briefcase with me, although I believe some of the other men might have been laughing at this fact. The lecture turned out to be of a basic nature, although the information was reasonably handled and for the most part correct. Afterward we all moved out to the clubhouse lounge, where soda pop and cookies were served and the weekend's teams were posted. Mr. Peters and I were on the same team, as I have noted. He was written in at shortstop and I at third base. This of course was an insult to me but I was not bothered by it. Various members of the team were introducing themselves to one another, and I did not want to appear slighted at this early juncture. It was bad enough that I was carrying a briefcase. Mr. Peters took off his baseball cap, slapped me on the back with it, and made a comment about it being like old times; of course I had to agree, although I was not sure whether he was referring to our positions in the infield or what we each held in our hands. His mood was expansive, however, and after the cookies we walked back together across the fields to the hotel.

We went into the lounge for a drink. Several of the men had preceded our arrival, joking as we entered about "milk and cookies" and the fact that we were "in training," yet at the same time sipping cocktails from the hotel's expensive tumblers. The one thing I have admired about Mr. Peters since we were children is his ease with all sorts of people, and now again I was impressed with how he moved among this group. He shook hands, told a joke here, laughed at one there. It has not eluded me that this has been a key element to his success in business, and perhaps such ease is as important in the final analysis as my own hard work has been.

Shortly, I found myself without conversation, and not knowing what else to do I moved to the window with my drink, where I pretended to stare out at the fields. The room was reflected in the glass, and I used the opportunity to study Mr. Peters's movements among the other players. I do not know whether the men turned to him because of his success in the marketplace or whether his success in the marketplace in fact resulted from the fact that men turned to him, but it was clear that he commanded attention. I myself have never done so. Many of those present in this lounge were successful in their own right, some hugely so, yet Mr. Peters could have spoken to any of them he wished.

However, within a short space of time, he left a group he was speaking with, came directly to the window, and stood next to me. "A nice view," he said.

"You see some interesting things from here," I answered.

He commented on the line drive I had hit earlier, and I answered by complimenting him on a double play he had turned, although in truth I thought he had been early on the pivot. We stood looking over the lighted fields, clinking the ice in our tumblers. I had been expecting a business proposal, and this was when it was made.

"Look, Roth," he said, putting his arm around my shoulder, "we're not happy with our bean counters anymore."

I will admit I had been anticipating more of a cat-and-mouse game than this, and I must say that I was caught unawares. "Yes?" I said.

"Well, I want you to make me a proposal. I want Priebe, Emond & Farmer to handle our books. Can you do it?"

I looked out the window, trying to appear pensive, although one can imagine the satisfaction I felt at being proved correct in my hypothesis. At this point, of course, I was grateful for the kind of preparatory habits that had resulted in my having access to my briefcase at this moment. I smiled broadly at Mr. Peters, tapped the leather case, and told him I had already prepared exactly such a proposal.

He smiled at me, first humorously, then skeptically, then appreciatively. "Of course, Roth," he said, chuckling and shaking his head. "You've always thought of everything."

The fact was that indeed I always had thought of everything, because this is what an accountant is paid for, and when Mr. Peters suggested that we meet on the evening of the last day of camp to discuss my proposal, I happily agreed. Indeed I was quite pleased that he wanted to discuss business before we had even returned home.

Although the last day of camp was when the substance of our dealings took place, it is important to relay what occurred in our baseball games before then.

I do not claim to be any more than an average player, but something happened to me in the ensuing days that no doubt will not happen again, and that, I admit, had not ever happened to me before. I suppose it began with my sleep in bed that second night. It was deep and slumberous, the type of sleep I had not enjoyed in many years, and when I woke for our first day of play I felt I was a young man again. Our team was nicknamed the Sluggers, and that first morning we played against the Bashers. The Bashers were comprised primarily of a group of radiologists from a practice in Boulder, Colorado. I do not know how a group of radiologists became so proficient at baseball, yet within two innings they had scattered base hits to every field and gathered a tally of four runs, to none for the Sluggers. Their representative from major league baseball was Alan Gallagher, a utility infielder I only vaguely remembered from a number of years back, and our own was one Kent

Powell, whom I did not recall at all. Willie Mays, it seemed, would not be playing with us. Naturally this was a disappointment, but I will not dwell on it. Of some interest was the fact the Mr. Gallagher at his age could contribute very little to the Bashers' effort, and that Mr. Powell could contribute almost nothing to our own. He played first base passably and did not hit at all. The Bashers were led instead by a Dr. Argusian, who some years ago had played baseball for the University of Texas and was now in left field. He scored runs in both the first and second innings and in the outfield caught a ball hit well over his head.

Apparently our own batting order had been chosen randomly, and therefore I did not come to the plate until the third inning. By this time we already had the bearing of a losing team. Mr. Peters had struck out in the number-four position, as had three others of the six men preceding me, and none of our players had reached base. Therefore it was with some trepidation that I entered the batter's box and faced Mr. Corsetti to lead off the third inning. As I said, however, I had slept well, and as I dug in my spikes and loosened the bat on my shoulder I felt a limberness in my arms and an acuity in my eyes that I had not felt for years. Briefly, I hit the first pitch into left-center field for a double.

Although I was not brought around to score, that inning in the field I made a rather nice play at third base on a ball that had apparently been hit into the hole. Mr. Peters slapped me on the back, and Kent Powell paid me a compliment from his position behind me. Furthermore, I noticed afterward that Willie Mays now sat in our dugout and that he had seen the play. Needless to say, I was pleased. Two innings later I hit a nice ball into right field, and amid the general hubbub from the dugout as I made the turn at first base I believe I heard the specific praise of Mr. Mays. Although between innings he chatted only with Mr. Peters on our bench, I felt loose of limb and elevated of spirit and did not take notice, although it occurred to me briefly that Willie Mays and Eugene Peters had hobnobbed before.

It would not be inaccurate to say that my play had inspired the Sluggers. Our next turn at the plate produced a run and the following inning two more, so that late in the game we trailed by only one run and were in every way a rejuvenated club. In the meantime, Dr. Argusian had matched my feats. In the fourth inning he had made a fine catch of a sinking line drive that ended a brief rally for us, and in the sixth he had hit a ball to the wall in left-center field. It is to new heights that competition naturally lifts us, and in the seventh I myself hit a ball to the same spot. I can only say that some small change seemed to have occurred inside me, some quickening of reflex and sharpening of vision that allowed me to see the pitch as though against a background of black and to hit it as though murderous. The ball caromed from my bat and did not dip until it hit the warning track in left field, and by this time I was standing on second base breathing the bracing aroma of infield clay. The game proceeded neck and neck. Our opponents scored a run in the top of the eighth, and we answered with two in the bottom. Willie Mays seemed to be rooting for our side, and as we left the bench that inning tied with the Bashers, he slapped hands with Mr. Peters and spoke general encouragement to us all.

Although Willie Mays said nothing more to me specifically, I believe it is accurate and therefore not immodest to say that by the final inning the game had turned into a contest between Dr. Argusian and me. He had reached base safely four times in four appearances at the plate, and I had made the same percentage in three; he had produced a defensive gem and so had I. I had noticed that in their dugout the men seemed to gather about Dr. Argusian, and although the corollary did not occur in our own, it was easy enough to see why. Willie Mays sat with us through the entire last half of the game, and for all of us, I believe, this was like finding ourselves in a taxicab with the king of England.

Although it strains the credibility to recall what happened at the end of that first contest, indeed the final inning unfolded like the glorious dream of a child. We came to the plate in the bottom of the ninth tied with the Bashers, and Eugene Peters led off. Briefly, he reached base on a walk—the first given up by Mr. Corsetti; he was promptly sacrificed to second base, where he remained while the number-six batter struck out swinging and I came to the plate, as luck would have it, with two outs in the bottom of the ninth inning and the winning run in scoring position.

I would like to report that I strode confidently to the batter's box, but what happened in fact was that I suddenly lost my nerve. I tapped my cleats with the bat and noticed with dismay that all the men in our dugout, including Willie Mays, were on their feet. Instead of giving me strength, this sapped it. My stomach felt light and Mr. Corsetti's first pitch broke devilishly so that I could not even bring the bat to stir from my shoulder. A strike was called. It was immediately followed by another, and on the mound I could see a small smile on Mr. Corsetti's face. Behind me the men began to stir. I commenced inexplicably to think of the failures in my life, which seemed to rise before my eyes in a tide of regret and misdecision, so that even as Mr. Corsetti brought his hands together in the glove, I had to step from the batter's box and catch my breath. Mr. Peters retreated in his lead at second, and I immediately thought of the differences between him and me—that he owned a large and growing business concern, that he had enjoyed his life both then and now, that he moved easily among men, et cetera. Yet I have always been a man of will. I took a breath, and even in my weakened state I was able to summon a modicum of courage and take my place again in the box. Across the diamond Mr. Peters resumed his lead. I have been honest in this portrayal and I will be honest again: Before the last pitch of that game was even thrown, I had decided that I would swing at it, and therefore I cannot say it was anything more than luck that it sprang sharply off my bat up the middle into center field for a single. Mr. Peters crossed the plate and we had won.

The revelry was instant and boisterous, with several of the players slapping me on the back, Eugene Peters hugging me across the shoulders, and Willie Mays briefly tousling my hair. Afterward we broke for the showers. Standing among the jets of water, soaping ourselves with the lime-scented lotion provided in large dispensers by the management, the talk was in large measure of my feats. Of course I enjoyed this but was not altogether comfortable, as I knew my last base hit had been a fluke. When one of the men shook up a soap dispenser as though it were a champagne bottle and said boisterously to me, "To the Most Valuable Player," I nodded gamely but took it upon myself to leave the showers as soon as possible and dress again at my locker.

It was then that Willie Mays entered the room. He passed by Mr. Peters, who had just emerged from the tiled stalls, doffed his cap, and sat down facing me. I greeted him and went about what I was doing, which was folding my uniform and placing it into the team bag with which we had been provided at registration. Several men immediately gathered around us on the benches, and although they appeared to be occupied with combing their hair, restretching their leggings, and fastening their shoes, I knew that they were in fact listening to our conversation.

Willie Mays said, "You had the eye, my friend."

I thanked him.

He said, "You were in the zone."

I thanked him again.

Willie Mays said, "Shoot, you were."

Not certain how to respond to this kind of exchange and believing that he knew what had actually occurred at my last trip to the plate, I was eager to steer the discussion in a slightly different direction. I said, "What do you make of this man's pitching?"

Willie Mays said, "Watch his wrist before he throws, he gives away the curveball."

I said, "I will."

Willie Mays said, "Shoot, you hit the ball, brother."

I ventured, "Shoot, yes."

Willie Mays said, "You creamed that sucker."

I said, "Say, I bet they sock you at tax time."

I do not know why I said this. The smile did not vanish from Willie Mays's face, but it did appear to freeze. At that moment, another man passed us on the way from the showers, and Willie Mays held out his open palm for him to slap. In doing so he had turned away from me, and I found myself in the corner of the locker room gathering my belongings, facing Willie Mays's back yet unable to pass around him through the door. I sat down again on the bench and, conscious of the eyes of the other men upon me, unpacked my cleats and tapped out the dirt from them onto the concrete floor. For several moments I worked between the cleats with my fingernails, pretending to clean them, and when Willie Mays still had not moved nor acknowledged me sitting behind him on the bench, I pretended to be occupied with straightening up the small mess I had created on the floor. I leaned down and gathered up the dirt I had knocked about.

It was Mr. Peters who finally broke the silence. "Jeez," he said in the easy way that made the other men turn to him, "they may sock you, Willie, but I'd give anything to be in your shoes, my friend."

Willie Mays laughed, and in the general agreement that followed I was able to extricate myself from the corner, finish my dressing, and go back to the rooms, where I attempted to take my bearings. I still felt a residue of embarrassment from what had happened, and sitting down at the window I noticed that my hands shook slightly. I looked over the vista and attempted to calm myself. I allowed my mind to wander over the day and my eyes to rest here and there across the fields—on the left-field alley where my drive had landed in the seventh inning, and on the newly limed foul line where I had back-handed a sharp ground ball in the fifth. The diamonds had been watered again, and in the setting sun the raked clay base paths glistened like rivers. Needless to say, I was grateful to Mr. Peters for interceding after what I could now only think of as my "gaffe," yet I was uneasy as to what effect the incident would have on our business dealings, which were yet to take place. That evening I ate alone at a steak restaurant in town.

The next day we played the Bashers again, and although I will not go into great detail, I will indeed say that whatever preternatural strength had been visited upon me the day before returned as miraculously the following morning. Briefly, at the plate I went three for five and in the field held my ground without error. To be fair, Eugene Peters also gathered three base hits, although he made a throwing error in the second inning and a fielding in the third. As for Dr. Argusian, he seemed to have lost whatever grace had blessed him earlier and contributed almost nothing to the Bashers' efforts. Again we came from behind to defeat our opponents, and in the clubhouse afterward general hilarity was the order.

This was the end of the weekend, and that evening we ate dinner together with the comradeliness of soldiers and afterward rose at the table to make toasts. As can no doubt be imagined, I myself did not like to speak in such situations, and as one after another of the men stood to deliver good-natured barbs and heartfelt thanks, I grew increasingly uncomfortable in my seat. Finally, to my great relief, Mr. Corsetti rose, went to the podium at the head of the hall, and announced that it was time for the presentation of awards. Now, I should add that it was not until this moment that I considered the possibility I would be named Most Valuable Player for the weekend.

The awards were given in a lighthearted tone. First, Alan Gallagher rose to present the Rookie of the Year award, which went to the oldest player in the group, a former state senator in his seventies who had merely watched the two games while sitting in the dugout in his uniform. This award consisted of Alan Gallagher's own Giants hat, which he proceeded to autograph and present to the venerable old man, who had walked to the podium with a cane. Kent Powell then gave out an autographed Giants shirt for Most Improved Player, which went to one of the radiologists who had been coming to the camp, apparently, for over a decade.

Then Willie Mays rose. Although he carried with him a pair of black Giants leggings, his bearing was not and could not ever be comedic. He was too great a man. "Say-hey," he said at the microphone as the applause subsided, "These socks are for the Most Valuable Player of the week. They were the ones I wore my last season in the majors." He looked around at us, suddenly at a loss, then glanced down at his hands as the room fell silent. I believe he was near tears.

I did not necessarily expect to win the leggings, as several other players had done well also, and I certainly do not believe in premonitions, yet as Willie Mays stood before us with his head bowed slightly and his hands fidgeting over the leggings, I suddenly understood with utter certainty that he was in the employ of Mr. Peters. How my heart sank for a moment. Willie Mays was the greatest player of his era. However, he was of the generation of players who had made their mark before the astronomical salaries of our current stars, and thus I suppose I should not have been surprised that he had to make his own living even in professional retirement. No doubt I would soon be seeing him in a television commercial for automobile parts. "Seeing as he wants to be in my shoes so much," he said softly, "these leggings are for him—Mr. Eugene Peters."

Several of the men looked at me, and although I was grateful for their gesture I nonetheless raised my glass and pantomimed a drink from it as Mr. Peters blushed and rose from the table. At the podium he shook hands with Willie Mays, turned to the crowd, and held up the leggings one in each hand like trophies. Here was a man with capital in four western states, a villa at Lake Tahoe, and an enviable position in a shrinking economy, yet he was beaming a sultan's smile because in his hands hung two tubes of limp black cloth that were grayed with age and worn thin at the stirrups. The men applauded and so did I.

After the ceremony a group of us repaired to the lounge, where the talk turned first to major league baseball, then to politics, and finally to the economy, which I am not surprised to report was of concern to many present. A consensus was reached concerning downsizing and cost-trimming to weather

the current crisis, and another round of drinks was ordered by
Mr. Peters. At this point Mr. Forbes left for a few minutes, and
I could see him down the hall talking to the concierge and then
speaking on the desk telephone. He returned, joined the conversation, and a few minutes later the door to the lounge
opened and three young women entered.

Mr. Forbes greeted them and waved them to our table,
where he provided them with chairs and signaled to the bar-
tender to take an order. I rose to be introduced. I am a man
with children and it was not until I was standing that I understood what was taking place. From my position above the table
I saw that one of them was sitting quite close to Mr. Peters on
the red leather bench and was in fact touching him. I wondered
briefly whether this kind of behavior was the quid pro quo for
the untrammeled success that Eugene Peters had enjoyed, and
though I admit that at that moment I felt a bolt of envy, I also
understood that without children Eugene Peters would vanish
completely from this earth. I excused myself and went outside
to the telephone, where I called Scheherazade.

I told her that I missed her, then followed this with a phrase
we often used in the early days of our marriage.

"Oh, Abba," she said.

Next I spoke to Naomi, who greeted me suspiciously but
then told me about a young man who had taken her to the
movies and about a party dress she had recently purchased;
Abba came on the line and we spoke about baseball in general
terms and our plans to see the Giants at home when I returned;
Rachel spoke last and said she missed me. She was eager to hear
of my time at camp and quizzed me concerning my at-bats,
which needless to say I found gratifying. We hung up and I
returned to my rooms.

I could not imagine what was transpiring downstairs, yet I

suspected it would have bearing on our meeting tomorrow. Perhaps it behooved me to join my colleagues in the sense that fraternity is pedimental to the business relationship; perhaps, on the other hand, to stay away would confirm my reputation as a moral force, which of course was integral to the standing of an accountant. I am not unaware that it will perhaps be of disappointment to learn that I indeed stayed in my rooms that evening. I took the proposal documents from my briefcase, read through them once again for accuracy, replaced them in their proper order, and changed for bed.

Sometime after night had descended to its full blackness and the moon had risen in my window, I heard the elevator arrive and boisterous conversation issue from the hallway outside my room. Eugene Peters's voice crowed unmistakably along with the softer intonations of a lady's, and I felt a bolt of distaste for the man, who though successful spent his days hobnobbing with ballplayers and his nights cavorting with strumpets. To my horror a knock sounded at my door.

I ignored it at first, but it sounded again and I could hear the two of them in the hallway rustling like raccoons outside a tent. I rose quickly, crossed the room in my pajamas, and opened the door, feigning sleepiness. Eugene Peters stood there, well into his cups, alongside the strumpet, and I will only record the first moments of the conversation to clarify its nature.

"See, sugar," she said, "you woke the man up."

"Just making sure you're ready for business, eh, Abbot?"

"Indeed I am," I said.

"Please excuse us," she said, pulling on his arm.

"Abba doesn't need to excuse us, I've known him for forty years, do you, Abba?"

"No, I don't."

"Abba and I are going to make a deal tomorrow, aren't we, Abbot?"

This sort of embarrassment continued for several minutes until the lady, who seemed to be of surprisingly good breeding, succeeded in wrenching him away from my door and steering him down the hall. I climbed back into my bed and was able to dismiss the incident quickly, although it did occur to me that Mr. Peters was a shrewd negotiator and that this might have been his attempt to establish psychological superiority. Outside my window the sprinklers came on. Again I rose and reviewed the documents.

In the morning we had our meeting. I dressed as though for the office—that is, in a neutral suit and striped tie, on the supposition that overgrooming was superior to under, and strolled to Mr. Peters's suite. Mr. Forbes, himself in a similar suit, met me at the door and ushered me into the foyer, which opened onto a second bedroom with a fold-out sofa and a dresser, next to which a portable meeting table had been placed. Here I took a seat. I had noticed several more closed doors adjoining the foyer and supposed these led to Mr. Peters's own bedroom and most probably another living room. I noticed no evidence of the lady I had met last night. Although the layout of the suite caused my own rooms to seem puny in comparison, I reflected that in general I prefer small quarters. Mr. Forbes offered me a drink from the bar, and I accepted tomato juice. I complimented him on his fielding over the weekend, and he nodded. He made no attempt to offer conversation, so I opened my briefcase and pretended to occupy myself with preparation.

Suddenly Eugene Peters entered from a side door, dressed in his bathrobe. He shook my hand, told me that he had one more urgent piece of business to attend to, inquired after my comfort, my tomato juice, et cetera, and left out the same door. Mr. Forbes then entered and rather glumly refilled my glass with tomato juice. He left and I continued reviewing my papers.

After several minutes I stood and went to the window. The morning sun was shattered into prisms by the blinds, and in the distance I could see a group of men on the grass. I was surprised, I must say, when I realized that these were the new arrivals here to replace us without even a day's interlude. Several of them were throwing the ball around the infield while another took swings on the pitching machine set up alongside the bullpen. The light and the long vista onto the grass reminded me of Fort Bragg, where I had spent a few months at the end of the Korean War. The man hitting on the machine missed most of the pitches or nicked foul pop-ups that flew up behind him and bounced in the rope mesh like birds struggling in a net. It occurred to me that Mr. Peters had worn his bathrobe for a strategic reason, and I removed my jacket and set it across the dresser.

At the window the man I was watching suddenly hit a string of low, powerful line drives that sped to the end of the cage and ricocheted off the restraining fence. In a game they would have gone for extra bases. As suddenly as this string began, however, it ended, and he missed four pitches in a row. I was watching this demonstration with some interest. He stepped out of the box and tapped the dirt out of his cleats, but I could see that he was looking to see whether any of the other men had seen his string. On the field beside him they continued their throws. The man put down the bat, switched off the machine, and jogged out to the field. He took a throw from one of the other players. Then he ambled up to the man playing third base and began to chat between the ground balls they were fielding. In a few moments he pointed toward the batting cage, and I moved away from the window.

At this point I heard something that sounded like a burst of giggling followed by another, lower sound, although as soon as it was over I was not sure whether it had come from the fields, from elsewhere in the hotel, or indeed if I had heard it at all. I was beginning to perspire. There was a great deal that made me uncomfortable here, although I shall not go into it. I patted my forehead with my handkerchief, went to the dresser, glanced idly in its mirror, and sat on the fold-out sofa beside it. Mr. Peters had been gone several minutes by now, and I began to wonder whether he really had another matter to attend to or whether he merely wanted to create the impression for business reasons. Again I checked the contents of my briefcase. I stretched my legs. The drawer to his dresser was slightly open, and without thinking I reached my arm back and drew out what touched my hand, which happened to be a piece of clothing. I do not believe I knew beforehand that it was one of the leggings of Willie Mays.

Yet that is what I now held, and although I suppose I should have replaced it immediately and closed the drawer, I could not help wanting to examine it. Leaning back in the sofa, I held it in my fingers. Though of course it was quite ragged, I do not mind saying that it was beautiful. The elastic top still drew firmly when I stretched it, and the stirrup at the bottom was of a second material—silk, I believe.

Though I knew Mr. Peters had in effect bought these leggings, as I sat there I nonetheless began to have thoughts again about the differences between him and me—that he hobnobbed with ballplayers, that he owned a large and growing business concern, that men of talent and ambition were in his employ, et cetera. I found it difficult to fathom that the lazy scoundrel I knew as a boy was now a captain of industry, and as I sat there with the legging in my hands I tried to remember if our childhoods contained some hint of our futures. At that moment, however, I heard him again in the hall, and without thinking I opened my briefcase and dropped his legging into it. Why did I do this? I cannot say I know. I might as easily have dropped it back into the dresser or simply continued to examine it, which was of course within the bounds of behavior. What troubles me is that my reaction was that of a thief caught red-handed, though of course my whole life had been spent in a profession that as a sidelight prevents exactly such behavior. I had little time to think. I closed the briefcase just as Mr. Peters re-entered the room, and this again served to reinforce the dreadful feeling I had that I was acting larcenously, although objectively speaking I do not believe I gave this dread away. Indeed for a fleeting second I had the bizarre thought that in another life I might indeed have made a competent thief.

Mr. Forbes had come in alongside. The two of them shook hands with me again and we all took places at the table, Mr. Peters across from me and Mr. Forbes beside. I set the briefcase between us—and again my own behavior surprised me, for one needs not have read a great many crime novels to know this was exactly the sort of brazen act ubiquitous among the criminal class. It was a feat of discipline that I was able to concentrate on the matter at hand.

I had never been in negotiations with Eugene Peters, and I was in fact surprised at the manner in which they began. He had changed his clothing, and now it was only I who was without a suit jacket. Nonetheless he opened by discussing everything other than what we had gathered to discuss. He talked about Willie Mays and the 49er football team, offered voluble praise for my performance over the weekend, and at one point mentioned that perhaps it was I who ought to have won the award. Naturally, I was pleased by this and denied vehemently that I deserved it. One can imagine my feelings.

Quite suddenly Mr. Peters slapped the table with both

hands, opened his arms expansively, and said, "Well, Abba, let's see it."

I was quite flustered for a moment until I realized he was referring to the proposal. Without willing the act I had at some point removed the briefcase from the table and set it on my lap, for that is where I now found it. I nodded and lifted it in front of us again. Mr. Peters smiled. I moved it forward on the cherry table, placed my hands on the latches, then withdrew it to my lap again. He was still smiling, although something quizzical had entered his expression. I considered opening the case on my lap, but to the side of me stood Mr. Forbes, who I realized was his henchman and would not refrain from peering into it.

I am sure that the reader would have chosen another course of action in this same circumstance, though I am equally sure the reader has not found himself in it. "I'm sorry, Eugene," I said, "but I have no proposal."

"I don't understand," said Mr. Peters.

"Our principles have determined that it would not be in our interest to represent your companies. We no longer wish to solicit your account."

"Pardon me, Abba?"

I hesitated to repeat what I had said, for I was in a dark woods and each moment stepping further into it. As soon as this phrase was spoken, I realized that Mr. Peters might well contact our principals for explanation.

Mr. Forbes had stood and moved a step toward me. "Say that again, fella," he said.

"We are no longer in a position to solicit your account."

"I thought you had the proposals all prepared, Abba."

"Well, I do not."

It is painful and perhaps pointless to recount the remainder of our meeting, or for me to relay how by uttering that single

phrase I had destroyed a reputation that had taken me a lifetime
to build. He asked me several times to clarify my position, and
in each case I was forced to argue against everything I had been
working toward over many years.

Of course, it would be less than truthful to claim that I did
not consider confession. Indeed, while Mr. Peters formulated
several rejoinders to my refusal, I considered opening my briefcase, attempting to cast the whole incident and business refusal
as a practical joke, and beginning our negotiations once again.
Perhaps this is what I should have done and let the chips fall
where they might—it is a tantalizing possibility to consider.
However, I did not. Our meeting escalated to threats and
culminated in rancor, and in an hour I was on the airplane back
to San Francisco.

Naturally I made every effort to put the incident from my
mind. I thought of what I would say when Naomi showed me
her new dress, and what I would tell Rachel about baseball
camp, and as we crossed the snowy peaks of the eastern Sierras
I decided that on the way home from the airport I would
purchase a small pendant that I knew Scheherazade had been
considering buying. Over San Francisco Airport we entered a
holding pattern, and it was not until we had circled the southern traverse of the bay, cocking our starboard wing toward the
banks of fog in the foothills, that I felt able to consider my
situation again. Indeed, it seemed that I had irrefutably dam-
aged the progress of my life, all because I had agreed to something I had not even wanted to do. I cursed the day I had
decided to attend the camp.

Shortly, I regained hold of myself. The airplane was crossing
the northern tip of the bay, and I removed the briefcase from
its underseat compartment and moved it to my lap. The man
next to me took no notice, and after keeping it there for one
complete cycle of our holding pattern, I ventured to open it.

The legging lay across my proposal. Of course it did—where else would it have been?—although I confess that I was surprised to see it. In my mind the events of the preceding hours had taken on a dreamlike quality, and before I opened the case I actually hoped that they had somehow not really occurred. Yet there lay the legging, coiled darkly across my papers. I glanced at my neighbor and brought it up into the air, where I rolled it between my hands, stretched it to and fro in the light of the window, and even smelled it, although the only scent I could discern was that of commercial laundry soap.

Suddenly the thought occurred to me that the man next to me might have believed it to be a woman's stocking. I glanced at him, but he did not acknowledge me. I cleared my throat and said, "It's not what you think it is."

"Probably not," he answered.

"It happens to be the legging worn by Willie Mays during his last season in the major leagues."

He turned to me, although I believe he may have been feigning interest. "Where'd you get hold of it?"

"At auction."

He held out his hand to touch it, rubbed it between his fingers like a rug merchant, exaggerated a sigh of impression, then turned back to his work. I was glad to have diverted his suspicions, although I will admit that his indifference jolted me even further, for clearly in my hand lay a piece of thin black cloth for which I had recently traded my career.

On the way home from the airport I bought the pendant for Scheherazade, although, as I acknowledged when I gave it to her, it was smaller than the one on which she had recently had her eye. Nonetheless, when I arrived home she seemed delighted. Rachel rode around the living room on my oxfords, and Abba appeared at the back door with a baseball, which we proceeded to throw around in our backyard. Only Naomi had not yet appeared, and when the afternoon began to wane I went upstairs alone to unpack my things.

In the bedroom I set down my valise and briefcase, put on the Toscanini recording of Berlioz's *Romeo and Juliet,* shined my oxfords, and proceeded to hang my shirts and pants and fold my underclothes. I stored the empty valise and sat down on the bed. The string crescendo of the second movement rose to its climax, and I went to my briefcase and removed the legging. I placed it in the back of my socks drawer, then removed it and set it underneath our mattress. Presently I retrieved it and hung it on a hanger in the closet, although after a time I took it out again from there and set it next to me on the bed. I thought of Willie Mays in the 1954 World Series, turning away from the plate and sprinting straight back to deep center to catch Vic Wertz's line drive over his shoulder. I thought of him pivoting at the warning track to make the legendary throw that held the startled Indian base runner from advancing. I picked up the legging and stretched it in my hands, and I thought of Eugene Peters when he opened the dresser drawer to pack. Of course he would suspect me, although he would have no choice but to suspect Mr. Forbes as well, and without admission there would be no proof. I thought of Willie Mays in the eighth inning on April 30, 1961, hitting his fourth home run in a single game, and in the failing western light of the afternoon my own ambitions seemed suddenly paltry. I knew, and I suppose I had known for quite some time, that I would never make principal at Priebe, Emond & Farmer. The position would no doubt go to a younger man. And while this was a disappointment to me it was not a great one, for although it is embarrassing I must acknowledge that within me I have always felt the impulse for uproar and disorder.

This, of course, is a secret I have always kept from my fellow accountants. Indeed, at the office the thought has occurred to me, more often perhaps than I ought to say, that I could just as easily have misadded columns, jumbled figures, and transposed tabulations as performed the careful work that over the years has been my trademark. Sitting on my bed, I was filled with a strange regret. This is what I had: a beautiful and capricious wife, a brooding daughter and an exuberant one, a son cut from my own cloth, a comfortable house, and a career that had proceeded reasonably well though not exactly as I might have liked. This is what I did not have: uproar and disorder, a life of music, and a future unfounded in the past.

Presently I heard steps on the stairs, and I replaced the legging in my briefcase. In a moment the door opened and Naomi entered. She did not greet me but went instead to the window, where she placed herself on the sill and looked out over the yard. I walked over and stood behind her, although I could not discern her mood and was afraid to lay my hands on her shoulders or to speak.

"You seem different, Daddy," she said.

I went to my briefcase and removed the legging. A strange ebullience had taken hold of me. "I stole this," I said.

She turned from the window and regarded me. I sat again on the bed, turned the legging in my hands, and recounted the story as the sun fell lower behind her. Although any man who has ever had girls might understand, others will no doubt think it sad for me to say that up until that moment I believe I had never in my life had the full attention of my daughter. It had grown darker, and her eyes, looking closely into my own, shone fiercely.

"I'm glad you did it," she said when I had finished.

I laughed.

"I am," she said.

"Don't be silly," I told her. Evening had descended quickly, and because in the presence of my daughter the darkness was suddenly embarrassing, I went to the desk and switched on the lamp. The bulb is a small one, and standing in its weak light with my daughter behind me, I was seized, as I sometimes am, with sadness. I suppose I was wondering, although it is strange for me to admit it, why, of all the lives that might have been mine, I have led the one I have just described.

II

▲

BATORSAG AND SZERELEM

In January of 1973, the year everything changed in our family, my older brother, Clive, competed for the mathematics championship of William Howard Taft High School, in Shaker Heights, Ohio. The championship was held in the gym, where Clive and three other finalists sat at metal desks arranged around the painted Taft Tiger at center court, working a sheet of problems. I sat in the bleachers with our parents, watching him.

Our parents had insisted I come. Clive's best friend, Elliot, was with us also, and at our mother's request we chose a spot ten rows back in the pine bleachers, which was close enough to see Clive's progress on the answer sheet but high enough to be out of his line of sight in case he glanced up. Clive kept his head down. He worked his feet in his sandals, while next to me, holding her breath for long stretches, our mother did the same in hers. We watched Clive's answer sheet darken with neat diagrams and equations, only the $+$'s and $=$'s clearly visible. Ten rows below us, Sandra Sorento, his girlfriend, leaned forward and fixed her gaze on him from where she sat, alone, on the first bench. Our mother's eyes kept wandering down to her, then snapping back up to Clive. Even from a distance I could tell Clive was doing well. He answered twice as fast as the boy on his left, and he only erased once, just before he handed in his test.

Then he came up into the bleachers to sit with us, and in a few moments Sandra ambled across the gym to the water fountain, pretended to get a drink, and then came up too. Clive didn't say anything to her, so I tried to smile for both of us. She smiled back weakly. Then she moved over and stood next to Clive, who was showing our parents one of the problems, set in the middle of a sheet of ditto paper, in smudged, purple type:

> LANCELOT and GAWAIN each antes a dollar. Then each competes for the antes by writing down a sealed bid. When the bids are revealed, the high bidder wins the antes and pays the low bidder the amount of his low bid. If the bids are equal, LANCELOT and GAWAIN split the pot. How much do you bid, LANCELOT?

Our mother beamed. Elliot whistled and shook his head. Sandra touched Clive's shoulder. I looked at the problem and pretended to think about it for a while, although I did not even understand what it was asking. Our father took it into his lap and said "Elementary, my dear Watson." He began filling in diagrams and crossing them out, tapping his feet and scratching his ears, until, a half hour later, the buzzer rang and the other contestants turned in their papers.

Later, after the winner was announced, our mother asked Clive where he wanted to go to celebrate. From the backseat of our Plymouth station wagon, Clive said something that sounded like *"Bayosh ahdj."* Elliot grinned.

"Pardon, honey," said our mother.

Clive said the same thing again, Elliot stifled a laugh, and finally Sandra said, "How about the House of Pancakes, Mrs. Messerman?"

We always suspected that something was wrong with Clive, but our suspicions were muddled, especially in those days, by his brilliance. He didn't talk much, and when he did, he used words like *azygous* and *chemism*. That afternoon, when our mother's electric blender went dead three hours before her dinner party, he repaired it using her iron and a piece of wire from our father's old shortwave, then went around muttering "liquefy, blend, puree, pulverize, frappe," under his breath. He kept it up. He sang it like a little guitar lick, all the way down to the end—"grind, grate, chop"—even while our neighbors from Throckmorton Street, the Goldmans and the Cubanos, sat around the dining room table with us. Clive didn't seem to know he was embarrassing himself; in the kitchen, where our mother had asked me to help serve the soup, she suggested I point it out to him.

In the old days our parents' dinner parties had been quiet affairs that Clive and I listened to from the top of the stairs, but now we took part in them. We sat with the guests and were encouraged to talk with them, and before our mother served the first course we would all join hands over the quilted table-cloth to close our eyes and say a prayer for peace. We were supposed to bow our heads, but that night I caught our father looking at Mrs. Cubano, and he winked at me. I winked back. Our father had a retired navy friend, Captain Byzantian, who now vinted his own wines in California and sent them to us, and when the Goldmans and the Cubanos looked up from the prayer, our father took out the Captain's most recent note and read it aloud. "A wistful elegy of a zinfandel," he said, deepening his voice, "a nearly human longing in a grape." He chuckled and filled the glasses. Then, while the Cubanos and the Goldmans laughed, raised their glasses of wine, and leaned back in their chairs, I told a story about how my friend Billy DeSalz had sent the same love letter to three different girls from three different schools. Mr. Cubano laughed aloud suddenly, and his wife, who I thought was exquisitely beautiful, glanced at him. I went on: But these girls, it turned out, happened to attend the same church. Now Mrs. Cubano laughed out loud, and the story began to take shape in my mind. I lifted my glass of apple juice, leaned forward over the table, and went further and further with my tale, searching for a plot that would take me to the end, turning alternately to the Goldmans and then the Cubanos, and every now and then to my brother, who was silently eating his roast.

Later, after everyone had gone home, our mother sat on my bed and asked me questions about Clive. She asked me why he was always silent at dinner and what the girls at Taft thought of a boy who knew why mica acted as an electric diode; she asked me if at school he and Elliot ever spoke the strange language they spoke in our house. Then, touching her temple, she asked me to multiply 3,768, our address on Throckmorton, by 216, our area code. "You can't do that, right?" she said, her eyebrows raised, as if there were a real possibility I could. "It's not normal to be able to do that without pencil and paper, is it?" She tilted her head to look at me, and when I shook my own, she smiled.

"Mom," I said, "I made up most of that business about Billy DeSalz."

She looked at me, quizzically. "I know that, honey," she whispered. "But at least *you* talk to girls in English."

It was not that Clive was mean, or dangerous, or particularly delinquent; it was just that he didn't know how to act like the other kids. As a junior, he had scored two 800s on his SAT's, while as a senior, when it counted, Mr. Sherwood called to say that he had scored two 200s. "It takes a profusion of intelligence to answer every question *in*correctly," Clive said that night to our father, who stood in the kitchen slapping the Educational Testing Service envelope against the counter. By then our parents had become used to calls from the principal. One day that year, Clive had stood still in the hamburger line at William Howard Taft, weeping, while the crowd of students parted around him.

The next night, while I was working on a plaster-of-Paris replica of Michelangelo's "Pieta" for my honors history class, I discovered Clive's secret. I was in the basement, molding my statuette on a piece of plywood behind our father's ping-pong table, copying the form from *Art Through the Ages,* when I looked up and noticed a sliver of light behind the Philco refrigerator box next to the furnace. When I looked up again the light was gone. I wet down the furled skirts of my Mary, walked to the corner, pulled back the box, and found, in the small space behind it, a cot and a candle and, dangling from hangers on the electrical conduit, girls' clothing. The box from our old TV moved, and Sandra Sorento stepped out from behind it. "Quiet," she whispered.

She stood before me in a yellow halter top and a spangled, maroon skirt that went to the floor, narrowing at the knees and spreading again at the ankles so that it looked like the bottom half of a mermaid; the halter showed a cream-colored slice of her waist. Things were wrong at her house, I knew.

"Well, nosy," she said, "now you know." She sat down on the cot.

"Were you watching me?" I asked.

"A little."

"I didn't do anything weird, did I?"

"Nope."

"Sometimes I do," I said.

"Well, you didn't this time." She smiled. "You're so cute," she said finally. "You're so serious." She touched her earrings, one, then the other. Then she said, "Come here, little brother," and slid over on the cot. She lowered her voice. "I *had* to move here," she said. "It was my only choice."

I nodded. "I hear you," I said. This was a phrase of Clive's.

She looked at me. "You do, don't you?"

I nodded again. Her skirt was threadbare at the knees, and I remembered that her parents were divorced.

"You know," she said. "I'll tell you a secret." She pulled back her hair, then let it fall again. "I like you, little brother." She smiled at me. "That's the secret. You and me, we have this connection, because you know more than everybody thinks."

"I can bring you food, Sandra."

She let out her breath. "That would be really cool," she said. "You know?" She stood, slid open the small, clouded window next to her, shook a Virginia Slims from the pack and lit it. "I wish Clive was as cool as you." She set the cigarette in an ashtray on the sill so that the smoke lifted out into the yard. "I wish," she said.

"I'm not that cool."

"Yes, you are."

"Maybe," I said.

She dragged on the cigarette again. "Question," she said. She exhaled. "Does Elliot ever bug you?"

"Me?"

She looked around. "Who did you think I was talking to?"

"I don't know," I said. "Not really. Sometimes."

"Well, he bugs *me*."

"Is that right?"

"Yeah, Clive is so superior to him. Clive's a genius, and Elliot's the last thing from one." She thought for a moment. "There's probably a word for what Elliot is."

"I hear you," I said.

She dragged on her cigarette and offered it to me. "By the way," she said, exhaling, "Did Clive ever tell you about us?"

I pretended to inhale. "About who?"

"About he and I."

"No."

"He didn't?"

I exhaled. "No."

"You're not going to tell your parents about me, right?"

"No way."

"All right," she said, "then I'll tell you." She met my eyes. Then she blew a smoke ring, and as it rose above her, she pierced it with another, smaller, whirling one. "I'm Clive's lover," she whispered. The smoke rings spun up toward the ceiling like galaxies. "It's a big secret," she whispered, "but now you know."

It was the year the Vietnam War ended, Spiro Agnew resigned, and the Indians took over Wounded Knee. It was the year lines formed at gas stations and Henry Kissinger won the Nobel Peace Prize. It was the year our parents forsook their religion, the designated hitter stepped up to the plate, abortion became legal, and our father wore bell-bottoms and purple ties. It was the year my brother spoke in his own language, won championship after championship, and began drifting away from us, until we began to fear that one day, like a branch in a storm, he would snap off completely.

Our parents were now Quakers. Our father came from a line of conservative Jews in Chicago, and our mother from Zionist farmers emigrated to Cleveland from the Negev desert, but now they went together two nights a week to Friends' meetings. They had spent a good deal of time that year adapting to the changes that were coming at them from every quarter, so that at home sometimes the world seemed utterly different from what it had been a few years before. They had forbidden Clive and me to watch anything on television but the news, and one night that summer when they returned home after a peace march and found us watching *Mannix* instead, they took us both downtown and made Clive get out of the car and hand the television set to a bum in a doorwell.

From then on we listened to radio news. That year it was bad. Gunmen with black stockings over their faces appeared at the Olympic Games. Israel was invaded. George McGovern, for whom our parents canvassed door to door, won in Massachusetts and nowhere else. In Paris there was a long debate over the shape of the peace-negotiations table. The day the negotiations started, Vincent Jump, one of the vocational students from our school, punched Clive in the ear and made him bleed, and our mother, who kept a map of Vietnam on her dresser, invited Vincent over to have our own peace conference. It was the third time Clive had been beaten up, and she wanted to know why. Clive and Vincent sat at our rectangular kitchen table, glasses of grapefruit juice and a bowl of whole wheat pretzels between them, while our mother and Mrs. Jump watched them from the living room. "I can't figure out what he does to them," she said to me that night, sitting at the edge of my bed again. "Why do Americans hate a boy just for being smart?"

Our mother never quite was an American. On weekends with her anti-Nixon placards rolled up in her hand, she would wait in long lines of activists for the Greyhound bus to take her to peace marches in Columbus; but when it came she would shove the protester in front of her to get on. She was damp-eyed, moral, and stubborn, and she felt the world deeply. Once, in the A&P, she browbeat a soldier in dress uniform, moving him up against the stand-up freezer and calling him *Chazer!* and *Gonef!* in a loud voice—a voice, I realized with embarrassment, that became accented with Hebrew when raised. I hid among the newspaper stands while the soldier, whom I pitied, stood blinking before her.

But she was devoted to my brother and me. In supermarket lines and at parent assemblies she called us her two geniuses to people she barely knew. Even later, when the evidence about me began to come in, she insisted. We were the only kids I knew who didn't know the *Partridge Family* plots and the only ones who could distinguish Cambodia from Laos. There were bookshelves in both our bathrooms, a fact that embarrassed me, and Clive and I were required to read at least one magazine each week. I read *U.S. News & World Report* and on Saturday mornings talked with our mother about what I read, eating wheat germ while she tried—I see in retrospect—to show me the bias of the reporting. Clive read *High Times,* which contained advertisements for pipes and rolling papers, and long articles about how to grow marijuana in the closet. He clipped the centerfolds, which were pictures of cubes of hashish or plates of diced-up psychedelic mushrooms, and kept them in his desk drawer with his guitar picks, his roach clips, and his collection of metal cigarette lighters. Our mother tried buying him a subscription to *Scientific American,* and sometimes she sat on the couch and watched him read it. Now and then while reading an article he would smile, and after a moment she would too. She liked to call him "cerebral" instead of "smart," which to me made his intelligence sound like an overgrowth, like a vine that would one day pull down a tree.

That week I tried to forget about Sandra in our basement, but I felt a relentless force urging me to confession. So that I would not mention her, I told our mother instead about the malt liquor I had bought recently from the Sicilian grocer behind the Busy Bee market; I told our father about Kelly Reed, whom I had kissed in the leather backseat of the Cadillac De Ville we had taken one night from Billy DeSalz's parents' garage; Billy was in the front seat, his head lowered like a chauffeur, and later that night we taught ourselves to fishtail on the wide, unlit road around the lime quarry; I told Clive about the things I had stolen that semester, candy bars and beer, mostly, and now and then a record. But what I really wanted to say, what took all my discipline not to blurt out, was that I had found his girlfriend, dressed in glitter, hiding in the basement of our house.

Instead, I tried to get Clive to talk about it. He had always lived an entire secret life that he would never discuss, but I did my best to put him in a confessional mood. It was difficult. He never talked about anything, about the senior parties he went to or the bands he played with in his friends' garages; he never gave me advice, the way other brothers did, about girls or dressing or mixed drinks. Every night that week I washed the pots and pans with him after dinner, and every night, standing next to me with drooping shoulders and tapping, out-turned feet, he dried them without speaking; hunched over the sink next to him, I could feel the familiar ease that passed between us, like radar, and I tried to let it wash over us so that he would talk. Yet in him it only inspired silence. Between pots he would rest his knee against mine and tap out guitar fret-work on the towel, but he would not say anything; I would plunge my hands into the steaming water and tell the half-invented story of my friends training a telescope from the roof of the gym through the one unclouded window of the girls' locker room into their shower, or about cheating on our multiple-choice geometry test by placing our feet on specific colored tiles on the floor of the math room. I told stories and looked into his eyes; I told them and looked out the window; but no matter what I did, no matter how much I talked or how silent I tried to keep myself, I could not entice him to talk about Sandra.

"Lover," I said softly at the sink. Next to me, I sensed Clive's little twists and nods. Of course, he and Sandra were boyfriend and girlfriend, but *lover* was a word I had never heard in conversation before, a word I could not imagine our parents, or my brother or anybody I knew ever using. It made it seem as if that was *all* they did. I let the hot water run until it steamed up the windows. Then I said it again, *lover,* with a little French accent, but Clive didn't answer.

After dinner I watched our father drinking coffee, our mother leaning over the counter, and Clive pouring unfiltered apple juice, but these actions did not distract me; they only made my secret more exquisite. I felt my chest expanding, like helium, urging me to confess. Clive picked at some apple pie;

I almost told him then that I knew. Our mother read her *Friends' News* on the living room couch; there, I almost told her. Our father went back to his office to check on his accounts. Our parents moved about the house, doing their chores, oblivious to Sandra hidden downstairs, like a body oblivious to its beating heart.

Finally, late that night, I went into our father's office and asked him to play ping-pong. "I just feel like playing," I said. We walked down to the basement, where he screwed in the light bulb, took the paddles from the bin where they'd lain for months, and dusted them on his pant leg. With the arm of his sweater, he dusted the ping-pong table.

"I'm not sure what's got into you, sailor," he said, patting me on the shoulder, "but I sure am glad to see it."

Again I almost told him. Instead, I held the ball in my open palm for a moment, listening to the click of the furnace and the squeaks of the ceiling joists where our mother walked above us in the kitchen, and then I said, "Service." I hit a slice that he slapped back hard into the corner for the point. The ball bounced underneath the stairs, and I retrieved it. "One–zero," I said. "What do you think of Clive?" I asked.

"Zero–*one*, sailor. What do you mean, what do I think of Clive?"

"He's been acting strange, that's all."

"Is that supposed to be a news flash?"

"I just thought I'd tell you." I showed him the ball again. "Service."

He laughed and returned it to the same spot in the corner for the point. "Thanks, sailor," he said. Then he hit another past my backhand.

"What about Elliot?" I said.

"Elliot's a fine kid, why? Is there something I should know about?"

I served while he was looking me in the eyes and surprised him. "No, I'm just talking. Three–one."

"One–three."

"What about Sandra?" I said.

"What about her?"

I waited a moment. "What do you think of her?"

He crouched to receive my serve, his paddle held from the back of his hand the way the Chinese players had held it that year in the Olympics, and behind the refrigerator box I heard the flex of Sandra's cot. "She's his belle," he said as I served, "if that's what you mean, but he'll get over her."

After he won the point the only sounds in the basement were our father's breathing and the soft rush of the furnace pilot. "I'm not sure he will," I said.

He laughed.

"I think she's kind of pretty," I said.

"Pretty, William?" He shook his head. "Maybe so, but it's a cheap kind of pretty. It's the kind of pretty that won't last. I guarantee it, sailor. Serve."

I waited a moment. Then I said loudly, "I'm sorry."

"About what?" said our father.

Walking by Clive's room one afternoon, I noticed a cold draft coming from beneath his door. There was no answer when I knocked, and when I entered I found him and Elliot sitting on the windowsill with the windows wide open. Their shirts and pants were off and they sat cross-legged in their underwear, like Indians, facing out into the snowy yard. Their faces were blank, and neither of them moved when I entered. Icicles hung from the eave.

"Excuse me," I said. "Uh, Sitting Bull?"

Elliot looked at me, then turned to the open window again.

His chest and arms were pale from the cold, and the black hairs on his legs stood up.

"Um, is this a physics experiment?"

"Shhh," Clive said. He didn't move.

"I get it. You're freeze-drying yourselves."

Elliot raised his hand and examined it. It was yellow-white, as though all the blood had disappeared, and I could see the tendons contracted inside. He dropped it back into his lap, where it made a sound like wood.

Later they told me they were practicing what certain monks knew. These monks, Clive said, lived by discipline. They were capable of sitting like that in the Himalayan winter, expressionless, without clothing, until they froze to death.

Clive's language had started out with a few words. One evening when our parents were out, I had come into his room while he and Elliot were playing Hendrix riffs with the volume turned up. Sandra was lying on the bed examining the palm of her hand. Clive was going off on a solo, bending his head up to the ceiling and contorting his face whenever the fingering took him high up on the neck of his Stratocaster. He pulled his mouth tight when the shrillest, warbled notes came bending out of the Heath Kit speakers on the bookshelf. His features, ordinarily thin, grew even thinner in musical rapture, and his hair bounced around his shoulders. To keep his eyes clear he wore a head-band, like Hendrix himself. Elliot—like all bass players, I had come to realize—stood impassively, leaning back with his eyes closed as he plucked out the deep harmony.

"Clive," I said from the doorway. Sandra let her hand fall. "Clive, could you turn that lower, please?"

I came into the room. Only Sandra looked at me. "Clive," I said, "I'm doing homework."

The guitar stopped, and after a few more bars, so did the bass. "Could you play a little softer, please?"

Clive touched Elliot on the neck. *"Aideshen sereti,"* I think he said, and they both laughed. Then Elliot said something like, *"Maiz,"* and they laughed again.

Sandra shrugged. I looked hard at her. "Don't ask me," she mouthed.

But soon they were speaking it more and more, at school and in the car and on the telephone, strange words that rose up suddenly out of their English conversation like jagged, prehistoric rocks. *"Kirahy,"* I heard, and *"Zenay,"* and *"Birkahoosh."* One day in the bathroom at William Howard Taft, I heard some of the voc-ed kids talking about Clive. I was in the stall. "That Messerman kid," one of them said, opening the shut hot-water valves with his Allen wrench, "He's a genius. I hear he invented his own foreign language."

But when I told our mother about this, she wrinkled her forehead. "Is this what a genius does?" she said the next afternoon when she lifted the end of Clive's mattress and an opium pipe and a bottle of Vaseline rolled onto the floor. "Is this the start of Albert Einstein's day?" she whispered, pulling open the window shades so that Clive finally stirred in the bright light and blinked open his eyes. *"Edj perts moolvah,"* he said.

I waited as long as I could. Finally I went downstairs and knocked lightly on the Philco box.

"I've been expecting you," she said.

"I brought some oranges."

"William of Oranges."

"They're tangerines, actually."

"William of Tangerines."

She laughed, so I did too, although I didn't understand. I took the tangerines from my pockets, set them on the window-sill, and watched her shake a Virginia Slims from the pack. "So," she said. "William."

I could feel myself blushing. "Sorry about what my Dad said, Sandra. I thought it would turn out funny."

"It didn't."

"I know."

She closed her eyes, held them shut for a moment, then opened them again and looked at me. "It's all right," she said. Then she added, "We have the kind of love your father doesn't understand, that's all." She smiled. "Tell me, William."

"Tell you what?"

She leaned toward me and tapped her finger on my wrist. "Just tell me."

"There's more tangerines where these came from."

"That's not what I was thinking of."

"I didn't think it was."

"I know what you want to tell me. I'm just waiting for you." She looked at me and smiled. "I'm clairvoyant," she said.

"Clive's going to win the Cities," I said.

"That's not what I was thinking of either."

"He could win the whole state if he wanted."

"William."

"What do you want me to say?"

She turned and looked out the window into the dusty, spiderwebbed recess below our deck. With her back to me, she said, "Is it true you think I'm beautiful?"

Our parents were trying to change with the times. During World War II our father had been stationed on the carrier

Ticonderoga in the Pacific, but now, one evening, he brought Clive and me to stand with him on the Carnegie Bridge and throw his old campaign ribbons into the Cuyahoga. He used to tend his insurance business in the dining room, but now that we had lost our television, he tended it in the den at the back of the house, listening to radio broadcasts of the Cleveland Orchestra. Our mother didn't want insurance forms in our living room anymore. Stored away in our old TV cabinet in a black steel box that locked with a combination were the cards he kept on all his clients, and more than once, when our mother was out, he had brought me in, tapped the sides of the box, and told me not to forget that this was our house, our family, our everything—that this was twenty years. In 1973 he was forced to talk about insurance all the time.

"People *do* have to be protected," he said that evening, rubbing his sideburns as we sat in the kitchen with the Cubanos again. They had come to celebrate Clive's victory at the Taft math championship and his upcoming entry in the Cities. "Insurance is *primarily* a service we're providing, and *secondarily* a task for profit."

"Why lie to your family?" Clive suddenly said.

Our mother looked up from her Caesar salad. "It's true, Simon," she said. "We all know what's going on with the military-industrial complex."

Our father set down his fork. "Since when," he said, "since what day exactly has an insurance salesman been part of the military-industrial complex?"

Our parents had had this argument before, and now the Cubanos looked down at their salad plates. Across the table Clive mumbled, "Grind, grate, chop, liquefy, purify."

Finally, our father smiled. "Anchovies!" he said, slapping his thigh and digging his fork into the salad.

"It's delicious, Rose," said Mrs. Cubano.

"It's a Caesar," said our mother.

"Anchovies," said our father, "are—if I am not mistaken—a dollar sixty a tin." He looked around the table, feigning surprise. "Thank you, Ohio Mutual."

Mr. Cubano laughed. Our mother stood up. "We could have eaten plain salad," she said.

"Right on," said Clive.

"What did you say, young man?"

Clive looked at me and nodded.

"Either part of the solution, Dad," I said, shrugging at my brother, "or part of the problem."

"Or dissolved in the solution," said Clive.

Our father studied him, then me, and finally said, "Insurance is about protecting the average person."

"Insurance is about corporate profit," said our mother.

The Cubanos looked at each other. Our father stood up from the table, went to the window, and looked out into the yard. Clive hummed a lick and shook his pick hand near his waist. Our mother poured lemonade into all our glasses, then sat again, smoothed her pants suit, and composed her expression. "Clive," she said at last, "William tells me they're pretty impressed with you at school."

"Here! Here!" said Mr. Cubano, holding up his lemonade. "To the champion!"

"I heard that some boys said you were a genius," said our mother.

"They know one when they see one," said Mrs. Cubano.

"Doofuses," said Clive.

"I believe that's *doofi*," said our father.

"They were voc-ed kids, Mom," I said. I waited a beat. "Everything's relative."

"It certainly is *not*," said our mother. "My two geniuses," she whispered, smiling at us. I looked to see if the Cubanos had heard her.

"Nobody said anything about William," said my brother.

"Clive, apologize to your brother for that."

"Sorry, William."

Our mother set her jaw. She swept her hand out over the kitchen, and her eyes watered. "Genius is one percent inspiration," she said, "and ninety-nine percent perspiration."

"Thomas Edison," said our father. He turned around from the window to look at her, then came back to the table, where he put his hand on her leg. "Geniuses *invent*," he said, fishing an anchovy from his salad and holding it out over the table on his fork. "That's the important thing. A genius isn't just someone who's learned something well. A genius is someone who's looked at the world everyone else has looked at, and he sees a new way."

"Or *she*," said Mrs. Cubano.

"Or she," said our father.

"A genius has to reinvent the world," said our mother.

"That's right," said Clive, "you can't teach a genius anything."

"Now wait a moment," said Mrs. Cubano, "that's certainly not the point."

"Geniuses study just like everybody else, young man," said Mr. Cubano. He sold tractors for John Deere.

"Doofuses," said Clive.

"What does that mean?" said our mother.

"*Diznaw*," he said.

She looked at me. "And what does *that* mean?"

"Good salad, Mom."

"Thank you, William. We're having macaroni after." She

thought for a moment. "Though I still say we could have done without the anchovies."

"Anchovies are brain food," said Clive.

"The point is that we didn't," said our father. "The point is that we did not do without the anchovies."

"What's brain food?" I said.

"Something you haven't been eating, little brother," Clive answered, and then he winked at me.

That year was the first Clive and I went to the same school, and in the fall our mother took me aside. "You and Clive are different," she said to me one day as we were tie-dying T-shirts in the bathroom. "You don't have to do the things Clive did." She dunked the knotted shirt in her mixing bowl, which was filled with yellow dye.

"How do you mean?"

"Clive's unusual," she said. "I just want you to know that. I'm sure your friends at Taft will be different than his. Your brother does some unusual things."

"Which ones do you mean?"

"Maybe we should use some magenta here," she said. "What do you think?"

I watched her wring the yellow from the cloth. "Which ones?" I said.

"Oh, ones we wouldn't be proud of. Things *you* wouldn't do. You know what I mean."

"No, I don't."

We filled the bathtub and hung the knotted shirts on a line above it, while she filled the mixing bowl with dye. I watched the yellow drip from the shirts and spread through the water.

"You and your brother are different," she said quietly. "That's all."

I tied up another shirt. "A lot of my friends shoplift," I said with my back turned to her. "Billy DeSalz got caught once."

In February the Cleveland championship was held, and our parents drove Sandra and me to the city library to watch Clive. The room turned out to be too small for spectators, so we had to sit on plastic chairs in a hallway in the library basement. Behind a metal door that had a small window in it, Clive and six other students worked at a long conference table. Our mother stood at the window, looking in, until the door opened and the proctor spoke to her. Then she sat back in her chair next to our father. "Why have a window if you can't look in?" she said. She looked at Sandra and me. "Why don't you two run along for a while?" she said to Sandra.

Sandra and I wandered through the basement of the library. The rooms were small and musty, each one furnished with a long metal table and folding chairs, like the ones in which Clive and his rivals now sat. Some rooms held no books at all, others were crammed full. Sandra went into one that was lined by rows of identical volumes in dull green bindings, and I followed. She gazed at one of the books, so I gazed at another, a thick volume called *Thermodynamics of Liquid-Gas Phase Change*, by Walter Y. Chang. I pulled it from the shelf and looked inside.

From the corner I could smell the flowery scent of her perfume. I scanned the chapters of the book, which had not even been typeset, merely typed, with a wide margin at the binding and the page numbers written out in words at the top, but I couldn't understand any of it. On some pages only two or three sentences were written and the rest was equations, full of symbols I had never seen. Sandra sighed. She said, "Wow," and a drift of her scent reached me again. "Think of Clive out there," she whispered, "doing stuff like this."

"Some of these equations are wrong, Sandra."

"What?"

"Some of these calculations are incorrect."

"Come on."

"They *are*."

"Don't tell me *you* understand this stuff, too, William."

I closed my book. "It's not that hard," I said, "if you know the equations."

She smiled at me and closed her book, then looked at me a long time. "My two geniuses," she said finally. Then she laughed and disappeared into the corridor.

I waited a minute, then I sauntered after her. In front of me the hallway was empty, and I moved along it, striding purposefully into each room, glancing around inside, then going on to the next. Finally, as I neared the main corridor, at the end of which sat our parents, waiting, and Clive, calculating, the lights went off in a room ahead of me.

"Genius!" Sandra whispered from inside.

I peeked in. "What?"

"Come in here."

"Where are you?"

"Close the door. Do you see me?"

"It's pitch black in here, Sandra."

"I see *you*, William."

I strained into the dark.

"Try to find me, William."

I stepped forward, imagining where the long table lay, struggling to see the pale shapes of the chairs. "I mean, Sandra, I just found a few small errors in some of the equations, that's all. Probably typos."

"Do you really think I'm beautiful, William?"

I steadied myself on the table. "Yes."

"How beautiful?"

"Very," I said. "Extremely."

"You can't even see me."

"Doesn't matter."

"You didn't really understand that stuff, William."

"Yes, I did." I moved another step. "Okay," I said, "you're right. I didn't. I pretended I did. I don't like thinking about that stuff."

"What stuff?"

"Equations. The things Clive thinks about."

She was silent for a moment. "Did you lie about anything else?"

"Like what?"

She didn't answer.

"Like, that you're pretty, you mean?"

"Yeah."

I felt to the side for the wall. "No way," I said, "not about that."

Now there was no sound, and I waited for my eyes to adjust to the dark. "How am I doing?" I said, stepping forward again.

"You're getting warmer."

"You're under the table, aren't you?"

"Nope. Colder, genius. Good, warmer."

"You're up on the shelves."

She giggled. "What *do* you like thinking about, William?"

"You must be around the *S*'s."

"Warmer. Hot."

I slid toward the wall in the dark, my hands out in front of me. When I reached the shelves, I felt for their crosspiece and held on to it, listening to her quiet breaths, just above me and to the left, like a panther in a tree. Then I said, "I like thinking about *you*, Sandra."

There was a flurry of motion, the hop of her soft landing onto the carpet, and then, from behind me, the creak of the door.

When I found her she was sitting with Clive and our parents, waiting for the other contestants to finish. Her knee rested against his. Clive was telling them that at the Cuyahoga County championships, which were going to be held in two weeks, there would be an audience, and it would be given the problems as well.

"We'll come watch," I said, looking at Sandra.

"William can look for mistakes," she said.

"The Counties won't be anything," said Clive. "It's the States I'm worried about. Sheshevsky will be at the States."

"Who's Sheshevsky?" asked our mother.

"He's some smart kid," said Clive, "that's all."

"His father's a physics professor," I said. "He's supposed to be a genius."

"That makes two of you," said Sandra.

"Three," said our mother.

Clive looked around. "Sheshevsky'll be trouble," he said, "but I won't see him till the States."

"Assuming *you* get there," said our father.

Our mother and Sandra laughed. So did Clive, and finally, so did I.

"Assuming," said Clive.

The next day when I came home from school, Eric Clapton was playing on the living room speakers, and I heard Clive say, "And now, folks, catch this." He was sitting with our father on the couch, and Mr. and Mrs. Cubano were on the two stuffed chairs. Clive's eyes were closed and he was leaning back into the corner of the cushions nodding his head, while our father sat forward at the edge of the pillows, nodding too. The song ended and Clive got up to pause the tape machine. "I'm turning the old folks on to Clapton," he said.

"It's not bad," said Mr. Cubano. "It's innovative."

Clive smiled at him. "You crack me up, Mr. Cubano."

"It's not bad," said our father. "The harmonies are standard, but the melody's innovative."

"It's just me teaching you what *I* know, Dad."

"I guess that's right, young man. I guess that's right." Our father winked at Clive. "I have to admit," he said, "you do seem to know a thing or two." The Cubanos nodded. "Now," our father said, turning to me, "why don't we all try the next number. William, come sit next to me. Rose!" he called into the kitchen, "Rose, come hear this." He closed his eyes, and I sat down next to him.

I moved as close as I could. "Dad," I whispered then, "my report card is coming tomorrow."

Without opening his eyes, he whispered back, "It came *today*, sailor."

Our mother appeared and Clive started the tape. We sat through "Bell Bottom Blues" and "Layla," our father nodding every now and then without opening his eyes, Mr. Cubano tapping his feet, Mrs. Cubano shifting hers, and our mother sitting at the cloth chair looking out the window into the yard. The tape clicked off at the end of the side.

"Well?" said Clive.

"I liked the second number," said our father.

"Hip," said Mr. Cubano, quietly.

"All *right*, folks," said Clive. He gave the peace sign. "What about you, Mom?"

She looked up from the window. "I have values and taste," she said.

"Birkahoosh," said Clive.

"Pardon?"

"Honey," our father said to our mother, "this stuff is all around us. It's the future." He got up and slid his arm around her waist. "We might as well learn about it."

She looked right at him. "You may listen to what you wish, Simon," she said. Then she turned to Clive. "And what did you say, young man?"

"Nadj a hoshaig ma," said Clive.

"Pardon, honey?"

"Nadjon melegem van."

Nobody spoke. Finally Mrs. Cubano said, "Tell us how you solved that problem with the antes, Clive. It sounded complicated."

"He doesn't have to talk if he doesn't want to, dear," said Mr. Cubano.

"Yes, he does," said our father.

"Djerunk."

"Honey," said our mother, "The Cubanos don't understand you."

Clive looked up. "Sorry, Mr. and Mrs. Cubano," he said. Then he looked over at me. *"Djerunk,"* he said again, as though I understood. I lowered my eyes. Abruptly, next to me, our mother started to cry, and when I looked up I saw that our father, at the head of the couch, had braced back his shoulders the way, in the old days, he used to brace them back before he hit us. But then he lowered them again. He closed his eyes. He kept them closed for a few moments, and when he opened them he patted our mother's elbow, turned to the Cubanos, and said, "Isn't it great what kids do nowadays. They reinvent everything. Clive's invented a language."

"Teach us a few words," said Mrs. Cubano, coming around the chair to lay her hands on our mother's shoulders.

* * *

That night after dinner I went back to our father's study, where he was listening to W-104 instead of the Cleveland Orchestra. "Afternoon Delight" came on, and I moved into the room and sat across from him on the corner of the desk. I could see my report card lying open among his stacks of bills. "What do you think of this music, William?" he said.

"It's all right."

"Clive seems to be quite enamored of it."

I nodded. "Dad," I said, "I just had a bad semester."

"Don't sweat it, sailor," he said. "At ease." He tugged at his belt. Then he said, "All this business with your brother, you know—the things he does, the music and the language—I want you to know that he's just trying to understand his life, that's all." He looked out the window at the Cubanos' house across the way, where the downstairs light went off and the staircase one came on. "Do you understand what I'm saying?"

"Yes."

"I knew you would." He fingered his sideburns. "Now, I'm not saying the things he does are bad. And if you want to do them yourself someday, why, that's just fine."

"It is?"

"Yes. You know, my generation has a lot to learn from yours." He unfastened his belt, loosened it a notch, and refastened it. He walked to one corner of the room, thrust his hands into his pockets, pulled them out, and walked across to the other. He returned to my side and we looked at ourselves in the glass. "A fifty-year-old man in a purple tie," he said at last. "Look at me, William—your father."

I was wearing one of my yellow-and-white tie-dyes, and in the window it looked like an egg with a broken yolk. I was

trying to grow my hair past my shoulders. "Look at me, Dad,"
I said. "Your son."

He laughed through his nose. "What a noble creature is man,"
he said and punched me on the shoulder. He laughed again.
"Your old man sells insurance, will you ever forgive him?"

"I forgive you, captain."

He smiled. "I forgive you, too, sailor," he said.

Across the way, the lights in the Cubanos' upstairs bedroom came on. Then Mrs. Cubano appeared in the window
in a maroon evening dress. She looked down at us in the
study, waved, and pulled the shade closed. The faint dot of a
satellite labored across the heavens, and when I looked away
from it I could see that our father was watching me again in
the glass.

"I just want you to know, William," he said at last, "that
grades don't mean anything. I want you to know that. Why,
I'm proud you don't care about them."

"You are?"

"They're just an external source of approval for something
you ought to be doing for yourself anyway." He laid his hand
on my shoulder. "Affirmative, sailor?"

"Affirmative, captain."

The satellite had cleared the zenith now and was edging
down the far dome of the sky. "In a hundred years we will never
know," he said. He pulled his hand from my shoulder and
leaned closer to the window, this time looking at himself.
"Sweet mercy!" he whispered. "How my very heart has bled,
to see thee, poor old man. And thy grey hairs hoar with the
snowy blasts."

"It's not that bad."

He ruffled my hair again. "Samuel Taylor Coleridge," he
said. "*That's* what's important, William. Not your report card."

* * *

The Cuyahoga County finals were held in April, in an auditorium at Oberlin College. The three regional champions sat on stage and puzzled through their problems. Both of the other contestants wore ties and jackets, and one had a yarmulke clipped into his hair; Clive's eyes were red, his hair was tied in a leather headband, and as always, he pulled his sandals on and off as he worked. The other two boys bent to their desks and scribbled calculations while Clive gazed about, adjusted his sandals, occasionally noted something on paper, then looked up and thought some more. Mr. Woodless, Clive's math teacher, was in the audience, along with Mr. Sherwood and the Cubanos, Elliot, and Sandra, who sat next to me. After each problem, the contestants were given a break, during which the previous problem was handed out to the onlookers.

Mr. Cubano whistled when the first problem was passed down the row and reached him. He handed the mimeographed stack to our mother, who looked down but did not take one, and then passed it on to Mr. Woodless, who did. I took one too:

> Of twelve coins, one is counterfeit and weighs either more or less than all the others. The others weigh the same. With a balance scale, on which one side may be weighed against the other, you are to use only three weighings to determine the counterfeit.

Next to me, Sandra's hands were clasped together. I looked at them and considered my brother onstage, his thoughts whirling with possibilities, moving deeper and deeper into the secret area of his being where none of us could ever go. His eyes fluttered and closed, and I knew that he had answered the question. His eyes opened, and as he wrote something on his sheet Sandra's hands opened too.

At the end of the afternoon the judges graded the problems while the audience milled about in the hall, drinking lemonade; I tried to talk to Sandra about a Doobie Brothers concert that Billy DeSalz had gone to, pretending I had gone myself, but she was distracted; finally a bell rang, and we went back in to hear the superintendent of schools tell us that in mathematics the real winner was the mind, and the country, and the love of knowledge, but that in this particular case, today's winner, with a perfect score, was Clive Messerman.

The next afternoon, I filled my pockets with tangerines and knocked on the Philco box, but when it opened, Elliot, not Sandra, was standing there. Behind him, on Sandra's bed, Clive sat holding the Plexiglas smoke bottle he had made in shop class. It was designed to conceal the smell of a joint. "Well, well," he said. "Since when do you know about this place?"

"Don't worry, I haven't told anybody."

"*Servoos,*" said Elliot.

"Who was worried?" said Clive.

"Dad says his generation has a lot to learn from ours anyway," I said, ducking inside to sit down with them. "He told me that."

Clive nodded. His shirt was unbuttoned, and he reached inside it, retrieved a joint, and slid it into the housing of the bottle. He touched it with a lighter, then examined it; the smoke filled the chamber but did not escape into the room. He held it up to the light for us to inspect. "Like a drum," he said.

"Like a clam's ass," said Elliot.

"I just came down here to bring Sandra some food, you guys."

Elliot laughed. "Feeding the monster," he said.

Clive nodded, then leaned forward and sucked hard on the bottle, clearing the dense smoke like a vacuum. "What else did Dad say?" he rasped.

I thought for a moment. "He said he thinks you're just trying to understand life." Clive laughed, spraying a jet of smoke from his nostrils that he tried to direct out the window.

"I hear you," I said.

Elliot took the bottle, waited for the smoke to gather again, then toked from it, turned to Clive, and said, "It's true, you know. William's right. We have to lead our parents through this stuff. If they don't see something, we have to show them. It's up to us."

Clive shook his head. "It ain't up to us," he said.

Elliot handed the bottle to me, and I pretended to take a drag through the top. I held the smoke in my mouth without inhaling.

"We have to educate them," Elliot said.

"Hold it in, William," said Clive.

Upstairs the back door opened, and when the two of them looked out the window under the deck, I quickly exhaled. "Supposedly you guys have your own dictionary," I said.

"Who told you that?" said Elliot.

"I heard at school."

"Kipihenni magayat," Clive said.

"Well, not yet, William," said Elliot. He hummed a quick Jefferson Airplane lick. "But we're getting there. We're writing one." He handed me the bottle again, and I took a small toke into my mouth.

"A whole dictionary?"

"Yeah."

"Who's we?" I said.

"Don't talk," said Clive. "Hold it in."

Elliot looked at him again. "It's up to us to educate them," he said.

"Nothing's up to us," said Clive.

That night, early in the bluest hour of morning, I woke and found Sandra sitting at the end of my bed. "Easy, tiger," she whispered.

"How long have you been here?"

She put her hand on the blankets over my ankle. "Not long. I was watching you."

"Was I snoring?"

"You sleep like an angel."

"Clive says I snore."

"Well, you don't."

I lay back down. She hummed a few notes. "William," she whispered, "have you told your parents about me?"

"No way."

"Are you sure?"

"Positive."

"Well, I think your mother knows. She looks at me like she does."

"Sandra," I said. "There is no way in the world that my mother knows about you."

She smiled in the moonlight. Then I heard her shoes drop onto my area rug, one then the other. "I *told* you I was clairvoyant," she said.

"About what?"

"About this. I knew this would happen." I smiled, and suddenly she was lying next to me, on top of the blankets. She draped her arm over my chest. "You're sweet," she said, "for not telling them."

"Thanks."

"You smell like your brother."

"I do not."

"Yes, you do."

"Well, he learned it from me."

She giggled, then we both went silent, and it took her a long time, lying there looking at the moonswept walls with me, listening, I think, to my breathing, before she turned her head abruptly and kissed me on the lips. Then she turned away again. "Really—" she said. "That was sweet."

I thought for a while, then turned and kissed her back, harder, and in another few moments let my hand move to her shoulder. At certain moments I could not help thinking about how I would describe this to Billy DeSalz when I saw him: *She smelled like oranges,* and *her lips were as soft as margarine.* Finally she pulled away. "Oh, don't," she whispered, closing her eyes, "Not yet, William. Don't ruin it."

When she had gone, I rose and went into the bathroom. Sleep had deserted me. I brushed my teeth with Clive's Ultra Brite and smoothed a palmful of his shaving cream onto my cheeks. I turned on the hot water and ran his razor underneath it, then stroked it back and forth on my face in smooth, decisive zags. The mirror steamed and I cleared a blotch in its center, where I tried to see myself in the way I must have looked to Sandra. "Hello, sweetheart," I said in a low voice, leaning forward into the regathering mist. "My name is Ariel She-shevsky."

That day I began looking for Clive's dictionary. I looked in his room, the basement, and the backyard; I considered his charac-

ter, then checked in unlikely places, like the middle of the
bookshelves in the living room and underneath the silverware
tray in the kitchen drawer. Then I decided that perhaps it would
be in an unlikely form and not in an unlikely place—inside a
book of matches, say, or recorded on one of his tapes. I
combed through his wallet. I poured out all the bottles of
vitamins in our medicine cabinet. At his desk, I sifted through
his roach clips, his lighters and cigarette cases, his guitar picks,
his articles on home cultivation and Grow-Lites, and his smoke
bottles and water pipes made in shop class. From behind his
bookshelf I retrieved his envelope of love poems from Sandra,
which were all from Shakespeare, written out in her cramped
hand. But there were no new ones, and I had read the old ones
many times before. All I could find of his new language was a
torn scrap of paper among the poems that said, in pencil, *"bar,
baratsag, barki,"* and on the other side, in calligraphy, *"We
must teach them what they do not know."*

On a Sunday morning in April, in Columbus, Clive won the
western Ohio finals. From there he would move on to the
States. That afternoon for lunch we ate leg of lamb, his favorite,
and afterward our father went upstairs to practice brainteasers
with him. I washed the pans and then dried them, and finally
went to the living room to study geometry. When I could resist
no longer, I went upstairs to join them.

They were sitting on his windowsill, *The Moscow Puzzles*
open between them, and our father was gazing at something in
the corner of the pane. I came in and cleared my throat.

"I was just looking at the moldings around the window here,
William," he said. He looked up. "Have you ever noticed
them? They are made of a number of intricate pieces."

I looked. "Congratulations, Clive," I said. "I dried the dishes for you."

"Thanks, William."

"Clive's taught me a few words," our father said suddenly. *"Agglegeny,"* he said, and looked at him.

Clive nodded. *"Servoos,"* he said.

"Allat," said our father. He looked out the window again. *"Bayosh, birkahoosh, diznaw,"* he recited, staring out the glass.

Clive winked at me. "Little brother," he whispered, "The old man has just tried a doob."

"I don't see what this marijuana's supposed to do, William," said our father.

"You tried it, Dad?"

"Yes, I did, sailor." He winked at Clive. "Look out, Sheshevsky!" he said. Then he looked up from the window and shrugged his shoulders. "Bombs away," he said. I sometimes wish he had been a different man.

"Bongs," said Clive.

Clive reached behind his leg, pulled out his water pipe, and handed it to me. He tamped down the bowl with the end of the lighter and pressed the flame to it as I sucked; I held the smoke in my cheeks, then pretended to draw it into my lungs. I held it in my mouth until I couldn't anymore, then blew it out slowly and took another hit. Finally I walked over and stood next to the windowsill, where our father put his arm over my shoulder and stretched his foot across to Clive's shin. We looked at the moldings for a time, and then out the window, and our father tapped his fingers to Clive's riffs. "Interesting," our father finally said, "you didn't inhale, William."

"Sure I did."

"He never has," said Clive.

* * *

At dinner that night our father opened another bottle of wine that Captain Byzantian had sent us. In the letter that our father read aloud as he poured glassfuls for our mother and himself, the Captain included the history of his grapevines, which needed the exact climate and soil found in only two regions of the world. "That is why I have come here," he wrote, "for soil this color. Too many years on ships and you forget the taste of women and wine." Instead of "sincerely," or "love," the letter ended with, "In the earth we shall find the hidden source." Our father repeated this phrase, draining his wine, then went to the cabinet and took down a glass for Clive.

"Well," he said, after he had filled it and another for himself. "Here's to the champion. And here's to the hidden sauce."

"Source," said our mother.

Our father winked at me, drained his glass again, repoured it, and pretended to look back at the letter. "I see that you're right, dear," he said. "Well," he yawned, leaning back in his chair, "My wife is right, and I only have one son left."

Nobody said anything for a moment. Then our mother said, "What is that supposed to mean, Simon?"

"Why, I don't know," he answered, swishing the wine in his cheeks. "It surprised *me*, too. It just came right out." He swallowed the wine, smiled at Clive and me, then drank again. "Too many years on ships, I guess."

"You're drunk, Simon," said our mother.

"Yes, I suppose I am," he said.

But that evening after dinner his words returned to me. I was in the living room puzzling through my geometry when I suddenly realized that Clive was the one he was talking about, not me. Clive was the one he considered his only son. I heard guitar scratchings from upstairs, the churn of the dishwasher in the kitchen, and the broadcast of the Cleveland Orchestra in our father's office. I had always assumed that something was wrong with my brother, that something in him was dangerous and perhaps shameful, and that my parents and I were allied to repair it, but now, on the living room couch, I first thought of it another way, that I was the one they loved less; that Clive was aloof in order to escape their love, and that I was zealous in order to win it.

I was in the middle of a difficult problem about river current, which I had read over and over. I turned to the hint section at the end of the book and glanced quickly at the schematic diagram of a raft in a river, then turned back again and did more figuring. Outside, Mario Ceref from down the street was kissing a girl under the streetlight; his hands moved down to her hips. Clive had shown me how to do this exact sort of problem a couple of weeks before; the knowledge of mathematics resided inside him like an instinct, the way it resided in our father, and I felt a quick sadness again in my chest. But I made it disappear. From upstairs I heard Clive's steps on the floor joists, then his window sliding open and the tap of his feet as he sat on the sill-seat and bumped them against the house; I stared out the window and waited for his marijuana ash to fall in front of me onto the lawn. Down the block the girl had walked away from Mario Ceref, who was now pretending to kiss the lightpole.

I went back and knocked on our father's office. "It's me, captain," I said.

He was leaning back at his desk, and when I walked in he lost his balance in the chair and nearly toppled. I steadied him with my hand and went to the corner of the room, where I looked out the window onto our deck. The radio was playing W-104 again.

"Yes, sailor?" he said after a few moments.

"I thought that was cool, what you said the other day about grades."

"I thought you might."

In the dark window I watched his reflection as he puckered and unpuckered his lips behind me, then shook his head ponderously. "Dad," I said quickly, "What would you say if I got into trouble?"

"What kind of trouble?"

I paused. "Big trouble."

He narrowed his eyes and thought for a moment. "You won't, sailor."

"How do you know?"

He raised his eyebrows. "How do I know? I just do." He stood and came up next to me at the window. "Character is fate," he said, looking out into the yard. "Heraclitus said that, two thousand years ago."

"What if I changed my character?"

He laughed. "You won't," he said. "That's the point."

The deejay announced the hour and put on "Walk on the Wild Side," and our father and I stood looking out the window into the garden. The night was moonless. In the light from the Cubanos' house we watched a raccoon from their yard appear atop our back fence, scrape for its balance, then scamper down onto our grass, first its forelegs, then its hind ones, like a pelt-covered Slinky. It ambled across to the bin that held our garbage cans. "Hmmm," said our father, "expensive taste—it likes anchovies."

"Thank you, Ohio Mutual."

He tousled my hair, and I felt better. The raccoon reached its paws up to the latch, knocked it back and forth, then gave up and climbed back over into the Cubanos' yard. Our father switched off the radio. "All these creatures," he said, "going about their business."

"What a noble creature is man."

He smiled. Garbage cans clattered onto the Cubanos' patio, floodlights came on, and the raccoon bolted down their driveway. In a moment Mrs. Cubano came outside in her bathrobe, and our father swiftly turned off the light. "Shhh," he whispered.

We stood there. Across the way, she was picking up the trash and dropping it back into the can. Her breath clouded the air, and she pulled her robe tighter. Then she sat down on the deck rail and lit a cigarette. She smoked it gazing up into the sky, and after a few moments she looked around, shook her hair out so that it fell down her back, then put her hand on the belt of her robe.

"Pull," I whispered.

Our father smiled at me. "Don't move, sailor," he said. "We could lose all reconnaissance."

She looked across at our house.

"Stealth is utmost, captain."

We watched, still as trees. After a time, she stood, tightened her robe, threw her cigarette butt into our yard, and walked back into the house.

"Oh, well," said our father.

He turned on the radio again. "Bad, Bad Leroy Brown" was playing. "You know, captain," I said, "Clive wouldn't have been interested in that."

"In what?"

"In what we just saw."

He rubbed my head. "He's not a sailor," he said.

"That's it," I said. Across the way, the light in the Cubanos' kitchen came on. "Dad," I said, "What were *you* like in high school?"

"What was *I* like?"

"Were you a screw-off? Did you care about your grades?"

"We were at war in those days, William." He went to his desk, took out his key ring, tossed it in the air and caught it. "In geometry," he said, "we learned bomb trajectories. Yes, I cared about my grades, William. Then I went to war."

"You can be smart without being smart," I said.

He nodded at me.

"Clive, William," called our mother. "Dessert! We're having pie."

I turned to the door, but he didn't move. He switched the dial back to the classical music station, then looked out the window. The raccoon had appeared again at the end of the Cubanos' driveway. "You're a sailor," he said. "With you, we've got nothing to worry about."

The music welled and the raccoon climbed back up onto their porch. "Do you recognize the composer?" he asked.

"Beethoven?" I said. "No, wait a minute. Haydn?"

"No, Albinoni. Listen to this. Listen to the passion of the cellos." He turned it up, and when the strings came to a crescendo, his eyes closed.

"Dad," I said. "I've been stealing things."

He opened his eyes again. "Oh," he said. "I think I understand." He gestured out the window. "See that deck, William?"

"Yes."

"That deck cost me sixteen hundred dollars."

"I know that, captain."

"Well, how do you think I earned that money?"

I pointed at his insurance file. "That," I said.

He looked serious. "Well, then, you must also know that what I said to you about grades was incorrect. Your grades are about as important as anything gets." He shook his head again. "Grades are all an employer has to judge you by. You know that, William, don't you? That what's right is right? That it's the squeaky wheel that gets the grease? You know, don't you, that these crazy times are going to pass?"

That week spring arrived, and on Sunday Clive invited me to swim with him at the stone quarry. He, Sandra, Elliot, and I snuck underneath the chain-link fence and followed the steep path down to the water, which was filled with a fine, rocky powder that the wind had churned into an unearthly opal green. Boulders lay along the shallows and the shore. Clive, Elliot, and I stripped to the waist and lay down on them, and Sandra pulled off her T-shirt and stretched out in her white bikini on the one between Clive and me. Elliot unpacked four squares of carrot cake and passed them around. I ate mine and lay back down.

Clive held his up and examined it in the sun. "Elliot baked them," he said.

I nodded at Elliot with my eyebrows raised to show respect. "It was good," I said.

"Kituno gomba," said Clive.

"Saipen," said Elliot.

I nodded again and smiled. I scanned the surface for fish ripples, though it seemed certain nothing could live in these waters. I tossed in a stone. "Thanks for inviting me, you guys."

"No problem, little brother."

I lay back down. After a few minutes Clive came over to me and looked at my face. *"Servoos,"* he said. He smiled. "It's a greeting." He laid his hand on my shoulder. *"Servoos,"* he said again.

"Servoos."

"How do you feel, little brother?"

"Great."

"You found our dictionary, didn't you?"

"Nope. I didn't even look for it."

"I told you," Elliot said.

Clive studied me. *"Djerunk,"* he said. He studied me again.

Elliot glanced at him. "Hey," he said. "We're going swimming."

"Skinny-dipping," said Clive. Then he pointed at Sandra, who was sleeping. He leaned up close to me. "You must have tired her out," he whispered.

Elliot grinned. "The monster eats a lot," he said.

Then they stripped off their clothes, and by the time I had stood up they were both up to their chests in the milky green water, splashing on the rock shelf a few feet from shore and jumping off the submerged boulders into the deep. I sat there watching them, when suddenly a haze dropped over me like a blanket. For a while longer I tried to watch them closely, then I lay back on the rock again. I glanced out over the water: they were paying no attention. Next to me, Sandra was snoring. "Sleeping beauty," I whispered in a high voice; then, in a deeper one, I said, *"Servoos."* But she didn't stir. I looked up at the sky, and thoughts of her began to drift over me. I could not shake them—the way she had blown smoke rings in her hideout, the way, in my bed, her hand had rested right above my heart.

I turned to watch Clive and Elliot again. Out in the deep, they had begun wrestling, pulling each other down into the water and twisting to regain the surface. They separated and then both submerged, while I watched from shore for their forms in the choppy green. They did not reappear. I sat up, and finally, near the ledge, Elliot surfaced. In a moment Clive did too, shaking his head like a dog and spitting out a rainbow. I saw the colors of it fantastically clearly, the indigo and violet fanning out from his whirling head, hanging in the air. They splashed at each other, and again I saw little jewels of color in their wake. Then these disappeared. They went under once more. I stared out as the surface grew stiller, and then calm, and then glassy, and then they erupted in the center again.

They emerged and stood on the shore. I pretended to be asleep, and when I felt shade on my face I opened my eyes and found Clive standing over me. *"Servoos,"* he said.

"Servoos."

"How do you feel, little brother?"

"Great."

He looked down at me, his cheeks streaked with quarry sediment that contained the palest trace of bright opal. "I told you, *bayosh*," he said, turning to Elliot. "You baked them too long."

They dried themselves with their shirts, whispering a few words in their language while I listened with my eyes closed. Sandra still slept, waking now and then to turn herself over. I heard Clive and Elliot wringing out their hair and lying down on the rocks, and then the small, steady splash of pebbles being tossed into the water and Clive humming a Clapton lick between throws. Lethargy welled over me. Just before I slept I was aware of all the smallest sounds of the quarry—the tiny chime of lapping waves, my brother's humming, the occasional groan of rock shifting in the heat and the plink of pebbles in the water. Sandra snored, just slightly. When I woke the sun was gone.

Clive and Elliot and Sandra were gone also. I stood and rubbed my eyes and looked out over the water, which had turned dark and was ruffled by wind; gusts darted across it like flocks of birds. I sauntered to the edge and looked around. They had taken their clothes with them, too. Evening was falling, and disappointment chilled me. I tossed rocks into the water, one by one, gazing at the choppy, gray shallows as they began to go black.

"The genius in thought," Sandra said behind me. I turned around and she was standing in her T-shirt and bikini bottom, smiling. "I was walking," she said, "but they're gone."

"Where to?"

"Good question." She stepped closer and I saw that her T-shirt was wet through. "I waited for you," she said.

"I guess you did."

She climbed onto a flat slab of rock and patted the spot next to her. I sat. "Tell me something," she said. "What are you going to think of me in ten years?"

"In ten years?" I said. "In 1983?"

"Shhh," she said.

This time her hands moved to my hips, then my belt, and at that moment I became aware of a line I had never crossed, then crossed it. I tried to remember everything so I could tell Billy DeSalz. I was also trying to work her bikini bottom down over her legs without drawing her attention to it, when she stopped, kissed me, and just like that, pulled off her T-shirt and top. Her breasts bounced into the pale light and I leaned up and kissed them. *They were like warm melons,* I decided to tell Billy. She shook the bikini bottom the rest of the way down her legs, kicking it off finally so that it flew into the air and hit on the gravel shore next to us. I moved my hands to her belly. *Her skin was like cream.* I pulled off my own shirt, stood and removed my trunks, and when she lay down again I shrugged, looked quickly at her so that I would be able to describe the sight, and then lay down alongside.

That weekend, in Columbus, Clive faced Ariel Sheshevsky for the state championship. Ariel was a slight, long-haired boy, with a leather headband in his hair and a derisive look to his features, and as soon as I saw him I knew he would be trouble. He looked like Clive. Both of them answered every question correctly, and although the lieutenant governor of Ohio laughed about this as he stood on stage at the end, holding the bronze plaque that my brother and Ariel would have to somehow split, our mother wept openly. In a moment Mrs. Cubano did too, and then, next to me, Sandra started as well, her tears cutting trails through the tiny flecks of glitter on her cheeks.

"It's only a math prize," I said.

It was those tears I recalled that same night, dropping through their delicate path, as I stood in the kitchen with our mother. She was mixing batter for victory cookies. "Sandra's living in the basement," I said.

She stopped mixing. "Boys will be boys," she said.

I moved in front of her. "I mean, she's been living there all year. She doesn't go home. Her parents don't know where she is. They don't care. She lives behind the furnace."

"Poor girl."

"She lives behind *our* furnace."

She dipped the spoon in the bowl, twirled it, and handed it to me coated with batter. "Sweetheart," she said, "don't you think I know about Sandra?"

"You know about her?"

"Of course. I'm no dummy, despite what your father thinks. Besides, I think it's kind of romantic."

"Dad knows too?"

"No, he doesn't. And I don't think you should tell him, either."

I sat down, and she went back to mixing. "I want to ask you something," she finally said. She didn't look up from the bowl. "She's his girlfriend, right?"

"Clive's?"

"Yes."

"You mean, are they *exclusive* or something?"

"Yes, that's what I mean. Are they boyfriend and girlfriend?"

"Well, I don't know. I guess so." Then I said, "Yes."

"That's what I thought. It's fine with me if she wants to live in our house."

That evening, as I stood across from our father in our basement, with the ping-pong paddle in my hand, it suddenly occurred to me that all of Sandra's attentions had been meant for nothing more than to insure her secrecy. I don't think so now—I think it is more complicated than that—but that night, standing at one side of the cheerful green table, I did. "Service," I said.

Our father mis-hit the return and it sailed in high to my forehand, where I leaned forward and hit the slam. I hit it too long and it missed the table, bounced once on the concrete floor, and skipped through the crack by the Philco box into her hideout. Our father put down his paddle and went after it.

If the spring of 1973 had taken place ten years later, I sometimes think, we might still have been at peace today, as we were then. Over the years my brother became a college physics professor and a dean of students, and I became a reporter and now, recently, an editor, at *The Boston Globe.* A year ago, walking on the boardwalk where I was vacationing at Cape Cod, I came upon two middle-aged women, high-cheeked and ruddy, and as I passed by I heard one of them say to the other, *"Servoos!";* I stopped and asked what language they were speaking, and I suppose they must have assumed, from the tears that came to my eyes, that I, too, had some knowledge of Hungarian. It was difficult to explain to them that I did not. That afternoon I searched through bookstores until I found a Hungarian dictionary, and I spent the night looking through it.

But by then it was too late. As adults my brother and I had become tender and comradely with each other, like soldiers from the same battle, and we finally grew to talk to each other in almost the way I had hoped we would. We lived in different cities, but whenever we saw each other there was an ease between us that I felt with no one else in the world; at Thanksgiving and Passover when we embraced at my door, I would hold him close for more than several seconds and breathe in his particular smell—a smell I have since, as Sandra did back then, noticed on the collars of my own shirts—and while my wife would move to the door to greet his lover—it is a word I have learned to use—he would whisper *"Servoos!"* into my ear. Although even then it was the only word of his I knew, I always whispered it back.

Things were changing so fast in 1973 that I admire my parents for trying to keep up. They were well-meaning people who were accepting what they could, one arena at a time, and I think it was a difficult period for them, especially for our father. What he found when he pulled back the Philco box in search of the ping-pong ball was my brother and Elliot, asleep on the folded blankets that were Sandra's bed, naked, their arms entwined. For a moment nobody moved. Then they began struggling with the blankets. But suddenly Clive calmed, and presently Elliot did too, both of them straightening their backs and composing their expressions until they sat upright before us, placid and still, the way monks sat as they froze to death.

"Batorsag," my brother said.

"Szerelem," said Elliot.

Our father's arm flashed, and Clive flew back from the

impact of the blow, hitting the wall with the loose wings of his shoulders and then crumpling. Elliot hugged his knees. Clive shook his head and let his mouth fall open, and then he turned to me standing behind our father with the ping-pong paddle in my hand. Flecks of blood streaked his tongue. Our father held his right hand in his left. Upstairs, our mother said, "Clive, William, dinner! We're having macaroni."

Then our father moved quickly to his knees, and though nobody in our family had ever prayed before, so far as I knew, that was what he did; he prayed, leaning forward and clasping his two hands together in the hollow of his neck, his eyes closed, on his knees on the rolled blankets; and then my brother, the genius, the dope-smoker, the disguiser of languages, my brother the faggot leaned forward too, but he did not put his hands together. He merely lowered his head, and then Elliot did the same, and I knew from their nodding that they were weeping. I recognized with something like the profundity of religion that this was a sea change in our family and the great unturning of my brother's life, and though I moved to my knees as well and put down the paddle, I felt no tears. All I could think of was that now was the beginning of my own ascendence. For so long, I had known something was going to happen to Clive, and finally it had. The inevitability of it had always been a half-hidden secret to me, a fact that persisted just beyond where I could give it voice. Now at last, as I bowed my head, I recognized it, deep in my own character, as the fleeting ghostly shape of a wish; and for this, fifteen years later, in a stifling room at Columbia Presbyterian Hospital in Manhattan, where the doctors told me I had better come on a late-night flight to say goodbye to my brother, I wept and wept and wept.

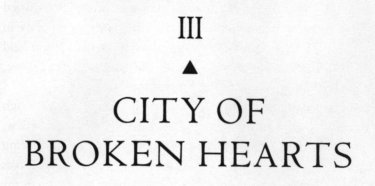

III

▲

CITY OF
BROKEN HEARTS

Wilson Kohler loved baseball. He thanked God for it, for the red basepath clay, the green grass, for the trim and piping of the uniforms. Gorgeous was what it was. It took his breath away. And he knew all about the game, too, the details of strategy, the pickoff plays, when to give a hitter the green light. At Fenway Park he'd watched the Red Sox since the days he had to carry his son, Brent, in his arms. Those were the days when Carl Yazstremski was still making his name in the majors, a bird-legged lefty with a funny swing; now Yazstremski had 452 homers and had retired, and Brent was about to start his senior year in college. He was going to school in the West, and when he called to say he'd be home for a day before flying out there, Wilson bought two tickets to the game.

It was the end of summer. The Red Sox were having a miserable year, mucking around in the bottom of the division that they'd won just two years before, losing games in every manner. Each afternoon, they went out under the cloudless Fenway sky and broke the city's heart. This is what the fans said.

The old guys, the women in windbreakers, they all liked to say that the Red Sox had been cursed since 1920, the year they sold Babe Ruth to the Yankees. On Yawkey Way in front of the stadium, standing with the sausage barkers, they said, don't put your heart behind this team. All they would do is break it.

But Wilson hoped anyway. He went once a week or so, driving straight to the park from work, and when he couldn't go he listened to the late innings on radio. His wife, Abbie, had left him three years ago, and he didn't have much else to do anyway. He played golf, took walks along the Charles River, and kept a small garden. He went out with women every now and then—women he met in the pricy bars around the Common or was introduced to by the wives of his colleagues—but the only thing he really liked to do, the only thing that didn't come mixed with bad feeling or regret, was go to the ball game. He parked his Lincoln Town Car in one of the expensive neighborhoods in Brookline, a mile from the park, and in the wide front seat he changed quickly out of his suit into white trousers and a short-sleeved shirt that he stored in a gym bag in the trunk. Then, the late afternoon sunlight filling him with its clear, river-washed optimism, he walked to the park.

He usually sat in the bleachers. Although he had plenty of money, he liked the public seats—it was something about being around all those people, even if he didn't talk to one of them. He liked the drama behind the big, green left-field wall—the lovers' quarrels, the toughs wrestling with each other, falling down in their tight Budweiser shirts over the pitched seats until the army of blue-tied bouncers reached them. In the Lincoln's glove box he kept a roll of five-dollar bills for ticket money.

But the day before Brent came home Wilson took fifty dollars to the park and bought expensive seats. Brent was going to be in Boston for only twelve hours, a morning-to-night layover, and Wilson wanted him to enjoy it. The seats were very good, in the low rows behind third base, and on the morning Brent arrived Wilson also went out and bought some younger-looking clothes for himself. In a store in Cambridge he found an open-throated cotton shirt that had been made in India and a pair of denim pants that closed with a drawstring instead of a buckle and fly. He wore his new clothes to the airport.

"Buckaroo," he called when Brent emerged from the landing gate.

"Hi, Dad."

Wilson moved through the crowd and hugged him. "Hey," he said, looking at his ear. "What's that?"

"Nothing," said Brent. He backed up and made an exaggerated show of looking at Wilson. "My dad," he said. "The hipster."

Wilson pulled at the drawstring on his pants. "You like?" He took Brent's duffel and they made their way back through the crowded terminal. Wilson tried to fall behind a step to catch a glimpse of what looked like an earring in Brent's ear, but whenever he slowed down to get an angle, Brent slowed down too.

"Hey, slugger," Wilson said, "What's the difference between a BMW and a porcupine?"

"With the porcupine," Brent said, "the pricks are on the outside."

"Damn."

"Maybe I should leave my stuff in a locker," Brent said. "My plane's tonight."

"You've heard that joke already?"

"Like, in 1979."

"How come I just heard it yesterday?"

"I don't know, Dad. How come?"

Wilson put the duffel down and raised both hands in the air. "Don't shoot," he said. "I give up."

Brent started down the corridor again, and Wilson caught up with him and ruffled his hair. In the old days they used to watch George Carlin and Richard Pryor hamming it up with Johnny Carson on *The Tonight Show,* and Brent would come home from the library with joke books in his schoolbag, but now Brent was serious. Instead of Notre Dame, where Wilson had been a Phi Delt, Brent had gone to a college in Oregon where there were only two marks, complete and incomplete, no fraternities, and no intercollegiate sports. He had done this although in every other way he had been a normal kid—a good athlete, a fair student, and something of a cutup—and although he had been accepted at both Notre Dame and the University of Massachusetts.

As they made their way through the long corridor, Wilson asked him about his summer job and his upcoming year at school. He didn't want to ask anything too personal because Brent shied away from that now, and he didn't want to start bantering too soon or the whole visit would pass before they had a chance to talk, which is what had happened at Easter. Brent used to be a talkative boy, but lately, for some reason, he had retreated. Wilson longed to hear of his life—it was, in some ways, his only news of the world—but he was aware that the more he questioned Brent, the more reticent he would become. It was not that Brent never spoke of his own life—every now and then he would burst forth with long accounts of his thoughts and troubles—it was just that Wilson could never figure out when it was all right to ask. All he could do, he eventually decided, was try to make him comfortable. There wasn't anything Wilson wanted to talk about exactly, but he wanted Brent to know he had a willing ear. Wilson had been through a hard enough time himself. He understood the importance of a willing ear.

That summer, instead of coming home to Boston, Brent had gone to New York City, where he'd worked as a volunteer for The Homeless Alliance and lived in Brooklyn in, as far as Wilson could tell, a commune. The thought of it now, as they passed the bustling ticket counters, made him chuckle. Three years ago on Brent's eighteenth birthday, the first after Abbie had left, Wilson had bought him a white Celica GT with a sunroof; now Brent was sowing carrots in a backyard garden in Brooklyn and cooking organic meals with six housemates.

"That thing in your ear," Wilson said, "it isn't a symbol for anything, is it?"

"Like what, Dad?"

"Like anything."

"Hey, Dad," Brent said, taking his arm, "It's the nineties."

"Sorry, buckaroo," said Wilson. He didn't know specifically what the nineties had to do with an earring, but he liked the fact that Brent had taken his arm. If Wilson had done the same thing, Brent would have leaped a foot in the air. Besides, he hadn't meant to tease him.

They passed a shoe-shine stand, and when the old black man there smiled, Wilson felt a bolt of pride at being arm-in-arm with his son. "Buckaroo," he said again, and he went back and handed the man a five-dollar bill. "I'm a lucky father today," he said to him.

But by the time they reached the parking lot, Brent already looked thoughtful. He walked with both hands thrust in his pockets and his shoes scraping on the concrete. "Hey, slugger," Wilson said, loading the duffel into the Town Car's giant trunk, "Did you hear that Abraham Lincoln was Jewish?"

Brent looked at him.

"He was shot in the temple."

Brent made a sound like a buzzer. "When are you going to wash this car?" he said, wiping his finger along the hood. Then he got in and put on his seat belt. When they were pulling out of the parking space, he added, "That was good of you to give the guy money, Dad, but you should have had him shine your shoes."

Last year Brent had come back to Boston for the whole summer and worked in a place called The Sanctuary, which was a shelter for battered women, and although Wilson didn't exactly understand a job like that, he had been happy to have Brent at home. He really didn't care what Brent did. He didn't even care if he earned money, as long as he was around. Since Abbie had left, Wilson's own life had come to a strange halt. Everything moved on as it had before—his job, his walks on the river, the bustle of downtown Boston; it was just that nothing of importance seemed to happen to him. He found he could not remember his daily existence. Once, right after Abbie had left, he'd sat for ten minutes in his office trying to recall whether he had eaten breakfast that morning. Soon after that he lost his car in the Copley Square Garage. But with Brent around last summer his life had started right back up. They'd gone to night games together, eaten sausages and coffee for breakfast, and worked in the garden. Even when Brent was out, the house was livelier.

It was not that Wilson always understood his son. In fact, he sometimes wondered who had raised him. Every Sunday Wilson had taken Brent and his friends to brunch at the Charles Hotel, and in between courses at the buffet he listened with bafflement as they talked about world politics or the plight of women. Wilson liked it when the conversation came around to girlfriends, and he made an effort to keep up with the names, but within minutes the subject was always back to politics. Some of the issues, such as paradigm shifts and hegemonic discourses, he had never even heard of, and he wondered what these Oregon professors were teaching his son.

The spring before, in fact, when Brent first told him he was coming home to work at The Sanctuary, Wilson had called around to his business acquaintances to see if he could find him a better-paying job. It wasn't a malicious act; on the contrary, Wilson considered it friendly initiative on his own part, but Brent got angry when he found out. Wilson didn't understand that. He knew enough to leave it alone, but it kept him up a few nights wondering what special sympathy his son might have for battered women. He couldn't help thinking it had something to do with *him*, and when he thought about this he vacillated between anger, which kept him awake, and loneliness.

His own wife, Abbie, had left a month after Brent first went away to college, and in the ensuing weeks Wilson had felt no desire to hit her, only to weep. He was alone in a three-bedroom house and he might as well have been alone in the world. After she left he had gone through a period of drinking, and in his office a few times—he was a marketing manager at an electronics firm—he had closed the door and sobbed. But Brent had come home that summer and told him about the growing numbers of women who sought shelter from their husbands and boyfriends, about the women who came in with bruises under their eyes or cigarette burns on the insides of their arms. He had explained to Wilson that the location of The Sanctuary was a secret, that he could not even tell *him*, his own father. This way men could not come to find their wives.

For a few days Wilson wondered how the wives knew where the shelter was. Did they call a secret number? Was it written in the stalls of their bathrooms? But Brent wouldn't say. When Wilson asked, he just shook his head. Wilson tried to tease it out of him. On the street he pointed to women in dark glasses and asked Brent if he knew them from the office, and one time, riding on the red line into Harvard Square, he asked the well-dressed woman sitting next to Brent whether this was the right stop for the women's shelter. When they got off the train, Brent told him never to say anything like that again.

There were other things Wilson wanted to ask. How was it possible, for example, to keep the location secret from so many men, and why did they allow Brent to work there? But Brent had become very serious about it, and Wilson realized it was better to let the subject drop. At breakfast Brent told an occasional story about the victims he dealt with, but if Wilson asked him questions, he looked back suspiciously. Wilson dished out the sausages, poured the coffee, then handed Brent the front page and took the sports section himself. It filled him with contentment to read *The Globe* with Brent in the morning, and he found that he could engage his son on the subject of the obscene salaries of major league baseball players. Then Brent would go back to the news.

Brent's seriousness about the problems of strangers annoyed Wilson, although he would never tell him so. He could certainly see how women had suffered great difficulty in the world, but he did not understand why this should be of such concern to his son. The female gender, it seemed to him, could take care of itself. It could more than take care of itself. In truth, it seemed to him that in the last few years there had been a secret communication among women, and that this communication was growing and leaving men behind.

Three years ago when Abbie had left, for example, Wilson discovered that he'd let his relations fall to the point where he didn't have a single male friend to turn to. He'd gone through his Rolodex. When Buck Hume answered the phone they chatted amiably for a while, but a few minutes after Wilson told him the news about Abbie, Buck excused himself to get dinner on the barbecue. He called Frank Scove in Belmont, his friend since Phi Delt days at Notre Dame, and Frank drove in to meet him in a bar. Frank was a good man, all right, but all he really wanted to do was get drunk and talk about Pi Phi girls they had known thirty-four years ago in South Bend. Wilson ended up putting him in a cab.

That week, idling his time in a bookstore near Harvard Square, Wilson had chanced upon a sign advertising a men's group. He had called the number, but when it was answered by a machine, he had left a false name. Two weeks later, on a Thursday night when the Red Sox were in Baltimore, he drank two scotches and drove to the address that had been repeated on the tape. It turned out to be the basement of the Unitarian Church in Somerville, but when he went in all he found was three morose-looking young men playing cards at a plastic table. He turned around and drove home.

That night he called Frank Scove again, but when Frank answered he sounded half in the bag already, and Wilson hung up the phone. He wandered around the house. In the bathroom cabinet he found a can of carpet shampoo, and he covered the upstairs rug with it and sucked up the foam in Abbie's powerful, self-propelled vacuum. He carried her empty bureau up to the attic and then stayed there, gazing out the small dormer at the wash of stars. The antidote to self-pity was self-improvement, his mother used to say, and he went downstairs and turned on C-SPAN. President Bush was speaking to a group of oil- and gas-industry executives, and though Wilson felt Bush was nothing more than a blind, self-interested man, when he took the podium beneath the presidential seal, Wilson inexplicably found himself crying. In the morning he woke up on the couch.

Abbie had left him for a man named Tad Heinz, a vice president at Wilson's company. She had left him for no good reason. On their last day together Wilson had taken her to dinner at a steak house, and she had explained to him that he had been everything she had wanted in a husband, that he had been stable and kind and a good provider for their son, but nonetheless there was something in Tad Heinz that she could not resist. It was irrational, she had told him, but there was an energy between her and Tad that was lacking between her and Wilson. Now that Brent was gone, she thought it was time to move on in their lives. Then she told him that the affair had been going on for two years and that she hadn't wanted him to hear about it from someone else.

This was when Wilson's life stopped, right after Abbie told him how long she'd been seeing another man. He willfully tried not to think back over that time. A few months back, there had been a phone call late at night, which Abbie had answered, saying "Mother, I'll call you back," and then she had gone downstairs; there was the weekend she went to visit a college roommate in western Massachusetts. Once, he recalled, he had seen her at the pay phone in a restaurant after she went to the ladies room; and it was a couple of years ago, now that he thought about it, that she had changed perfumes.

The night she said she was leaving him she drove home with him after dinner, and despite her objections he stopped at the flower shop; while Abbie waited in the car, he told Panos, the old Greek florist who'd been a steady source of cheer to him for years, that his wife was upset and that he needed something extraordinary for her. Panos winked and brought out a vase of sunflowers, foxgloves, and birds of paradise from the cooler, and Wilson walked out to the car holding it behind his back, reasonably optimistic that he could change all that had just happened.

Later that night, when she left, he sat at the table in the back of the house, staring at the flowers, so shamed by them he could not look up. He did not watch her go; he did not listen for the familiar rev and downshift of her Toyota; he did not plead. He sat for a long time in the breakfast room. Then he picked up *The Globe* and thought to himself, *I must continue to read the newspaper.*

In the days that followed he did not feel sad exactly, just blank, as though if he could not report to Abbie about the events of his life, they had not really happened. He cried for the first time since the death of his father, but the tears did not seem to come from sadness nor to relieve it. They seemed biological, and he watched them, like symptoms.

He tried not to think about Tad Heinz. Tad worked in another building, two miles east on Route 128, and it wasn't hard for Wilson to physically avoid him. Whenever he came to mind, Wilson used the trick his sergeant had taught him on the Korean peninsula—he named the state capitals in alphabetical order, from Albany to Trenton. But one day that winter, he turned down an aisle in the parking lot of his own office complex and there was Tad getting out of a metallic green Mercedes. Three months had passed since Abbie had gone to live with him and his two daughters in Marblehead. The day was bitter cold, but Wilson stopped the Lincoln and got out. Ruts of slick, exhaust-stained ice separated him from the man who had taken his wife. He found himself running toward him. Tad was locking the car door, dressed in a wool overcoat with a ridiculous company muffler rolled around his neck.

Wilson had already made the payments on his house and had saved enough for two years of Brent's college. He tried to slow down, throwing out his arms for balance and half-sliding on the ice, but when he reached the Mercedes he grabbed the flapping ends of Tad's muffler and pulled. Tad turned and saw him, and then they were both splayed on the hard, uneven ice. Tad kept trying to get up. Wilson hadn't punched anyone since his army days. In his thick overcoat he struggled forward, reaching for Tad's shoulders, thrusting down the well-sewn leather gloves that came up in defense, finally throwing his weight into a sharp right uppercut that landed on Tad's jaw. It snapped back, and Tad gasped for air. One of the secretaries appeared at the end of the lot, and Wilson had the urge to bolt, but then he sat back on the ice.

Tad held his jaw. "Abbie said you'd try something," he gasped.

"Up yours, Heinz."

Tad stood and got into the Mercedes. When he had turned the car around and driven it a few feet from where Wilson still sat on the ice, he opened the window, stared for a minute, rolled it up again, and drove off.

The next day Wilson went in early and packed his office. He packed his papers, the pewter inkwell Brent had given him, his books, the small bourbon flask, and the photograph of Brent at the beach in Cohasset, and then he went home to wait for the call from his boss. He stayed home the following day as well, but the call didn't come, and then the day after that, and finally he went in to work again and unpacked his things. He set them up on his desk and shelves and tried to work. Outside his window snow fell. Sitting in the wood-and-leather chair backed up against his desk, staring out to the fleeced January air, he realized that after he punched Tad Heinz he had expected Abbie to come back.

But Tad Heinz didn't even fire him. Wilson imagined his wife touching salve to the blue-brown spot on Tad's cheek, her hands feeling the newness, the strange angled shape of that jawbone. He wondered if she had really told Tad that he might attack him.

That afternoon he locked his door and wrote the first of his letters to Brent at college. In it he spoke of the weather, the Bruins, and the electronics market. He asked Brent about school and about his friends. He included two jokes about Vice President Quayle and asked Brent how many feminists it took to screw in a light bulb. After a few lines, though, he found there wasn't that much to say. He wondered what kind of father he'd been. The letters Abbie used to write Brent at summer camp were two and three pages long. "I was walking on Beacon Street," he wrote in order to reach the end of the first page, "and ran into Mr. Harkness, your old math teacher (divorced at the time he was a teacher of yours), so I took him to lunch. He sends his regards and reminds you to write out your division (fat chance)." He told Brent that things were different without his mother around, but that he was doing fine. "I love you and always will," he wrote at the bottom. "Dad," he signed it, and then crossed that out. "Wilson," he wrote.

He moved indolently through the traffic toward Fenway Park now, changing lanes occasionally so he could study Brent's earring. It was very small, a fleck of reflected light that could have been a diamond or a piece of silver; Wilson was a bit farsighted. In Kenmore Square after a game recently he'd seen a bare-chested man with a chain strung from his ear to his nipple, and at White Hen Pantry every morning he bought coffee from a girl who had a ring in her nose. She was a pretty girl, too. It was some kind of rebellion against that, he supposed.

One day he struck up a conversation with her and discovered she was a senior at Boston College, which was a Jesuit school, if he remembered correctly. They became friendly, and eventually he asked her what her boyfriend thought of the ring; she told him that her boyfriend was the one who'd bought it for her. Wilson poured his coffee and wondered about the world. She saw the expression on his face and reached over the register to touch his arm. "We're a different generation," she said to him, in a voice that wasn't unkind, and there was so much in that gesture that Wilson had the crazy instinct to reach back across the counter and take her heart-shaped face in his hands.

Turning at Beacon Street now, he decided there was no reason Brent shouldn't wear an earring, as long as it was a fashion among young men his age. It obviously wasn't true anymore that only homosexuals wore them. One of the chip salesmen at work had recently told him that there was a whole code among homosexuals involving where the earring was placed—which ear and how high—but this salesman was well known as a Neanderthal. Wilson changed lanes: Brent's appeared to be a diamond.

"So," Brent said, turning to face him, "Is there anybody in your life?"

"Drive, lady," Wilson muttered out the window at a car turning left. Then for a block he pretended to be distracted by the traffic. It always brought him up short for a moment, that at the age of fifty-four he would be asked questions about lady friends by his grown son. Brent was still looking at him.

"There are a few," Wilson said. "I'd give you names, but it's hard to keep track of them."

Brent said, "Seriously, Dad."

"Yes," Wilson answered, "it's seriously hard."

They were near Fenway Park, at the edge of the neighborhood in Brookline where he liked to leave the Lincoln at the end of a small cul-de-sac near a wooded square. He parked and was about to change into his slacks when he remembered he was already wearing his new clothes. Brent got out of the car. Wilson looked down at his own belly, now bulging comfortably against the unfamiliar fabric of his shirt—madras, the salesgirl had called it—and at the cotton drawstring that hung from his pants. He had imagined his life a different way.

In truth Wilson had been wandering among women. He had been married for twenty-three years and not only could he not replace Abbie, he still could not even imagine what replacing her would involve. Frank Scove, between bourbons, had once mentioned that for every year a man was married it took him a year to get over it. That meant Wilson would fall in love again when he was seventy-four years old. His boss at work, Herman Goldkorn, was only sixty-seven, and already you had to speak to him in his left ear.

He had probably dated a dozen women over the past three years and gone to bed with only a handful. The first, immediately after Abbie had left, was a young-looking stewardess on a Delta flight to Washington who had handed him a bottle of wine as he got off the plane. At his hotel he discovered the name Monique and a telephone number written on the label. That evening when he met her at the Capital Hyatt he saw that she wasn't as young as she'd looked, but the intrigue was still exhilarating. She was from Austria, spoke five languages, and told Wilson that he looked like a serious person. He was serious, Wilson answered, because his wife had recently passed away.

After they had drinks in the lobby bar, she invited him up to her room. Wilson was aware of having used pretexts to gain her sympathy, but as they sat down on the edge of her bed and looked out the window at the somber lights of the Capitol, his lie seemed to allow him into a territory he wouldn't ordinarily have entered. She had an earnest, attentive face, and he found himself telling her about his life, surprised that the lie he had told did not seem to alter his story. They kissed passionately, in a way he hadn't done in years, falling back on the bed finally and sighing to each other. Monique began to speak to him in French. He lay there, moving his hands underneath her silk blouse, imagining that he was indeed a widower and that the world had nothing more cruel to show him.

But the next day, instead of feeling buoyed, Wilson felt drugged. His meeting was not until the afternoon, so he spent the morning walking in the Air and Space Museum mired in regret and shame. The thought crossed his mind that from his plane reservation Monique could find out that he was not a widower; immediately he decided this was ridiculous. Later, as he was staring at John Glenn's claustrophobic space capsule, the thought crept into his mind again. He found himself saying "silly" out loud, and he left the museum and went to lunch, then for a long walk. Fortunately, the afternoon meeting involved all twelve marketing managers, and he was able to sit silently until it was over. He made a note to ask his friend Bryan Hannock what had taken place and then changed his flight home to United.

For several weeks after that he reeled. It was not the wildness of his act. He had been a wild enough young man before he was married; it was just that it was difficult to understand how in September he could have been holding his wife by the waist and waving at his son at the airport, and in November lying in a hotel room with no closer friend in the world than a stewardess from the international route. Again he found himself crying. He moved about the large house stuck between the idea of himself as a family man, which overtook him every now and then with wistfulness, and as a bachelor, which, unfamiliarly, made him ashamed. Buck Hume's wife tried to set him up with one of her friends, but he put her off. Herman Goldkorn's wife invited him to dinner at their house, which he couldn't refuse. The other guest was a widow in her sixties.

On a rainy afternoon in November a Trans-Am turned left too soon on Brookline Avenue and the Lincoln caught its rear bumper and spun it around in the intersection. Before Wilson could even get out of the Lincoln, a woman had emerged from the Trans-Am, already apologizing as she crossed the street toward him that it was her son's car, that she was so sorry, that she wasn't used to the gas pedal. "My God," she said when she got to his window, "you're bleeding." Wilson thought she was joking, but when she pulled her hand from his forehead, there was blood on her fingers. They were a block from Brigham and Women's Hospital, and in the emergency room Wilson gave Brent's name as his next of kin and told the admitting nurse that he didn't remember hitting the windshield. In an hour he was lying inside the strange, white CAT scan donut while the woman who had hit him waited in the technician's booth. Her name was Mary-Jane Donnelly, and she had argued with the doctors to be able to get in there. When Wilson emerged she waved at him and giggled behind the glass as though they were students together on a field trip. Wilson didn't know how to handle her, so he waved back, wondering whether this would complicate the insurance settlement.

But while they waited for the scan to be read, she sat outside the emergency room with him, and when it came back normal that evening, she drove him home. She parked outside the house and offered to cook him dinner, not even asking whether he had a wife or a family inside. Wilson wondered how she knew. She came on a little strong for his taste, but the doctors had forbidden him to eat while he was in the hospital, and now he was ravenous. He was even feeling a little woozy, although he wasn't sure if he was imagining this. She ended up cooking from what was in his kitchen cabinets, surprising him with some kind of Moroccan dish whose ingredients he could not believe had been in his house, and after dinner she helped him upstairs to bed and then got into it with him.

From the start she was a whirlwind. She cooked him breakfast and dinner and drove out to Route 128 three times a week to have lunch with him. On the weekends she arranged outings, and on Thursday nights they went to games together, where she sat knitting. Wilson was afraid of meeting any of their old friends. Sitting in the stands with her, he couldn't help feeling that their affair was illicit. Sometimes he found himself overly aware of his hands; he would put one on her knee, then withdraw it; he would let it rest on her shoulder, then the back of her seat, then her shoulder again; once, when a computer salesman stopped to say hello, he jerked it back as if caught. Mary-Jane Donnelly was energetic, but she was not graceful the way Abbie had been.

There was always something to do, however, and every now and then he reminded himself that the key to contentment was remaining occupied. Mary-Jane Donnelly walked around the house pointing out to him how he could change it. They painted the living room walls one weekend, and the next weekend she took him to a greenhouse and they bought plants for his study. She re-covered his reading chair, bought him a new set of plates, and hired a chimney sweep to clear out his fireplace. Then they sat in front of the fire, Wilson dozing off, Mary-Jane clipping articles from magazines. Once a week she sat next to him in the front seat of the Lincoln, waving her hands and squealing at the giant fronds that buffed and polished the car as it rode on tracks through the Rain Tunnel Carwash. He was hardly morose anymore. He wondered if he was falling in love.

One Sunday morning he came downstairs early and found her in the kitchen writing a letter. The thought occurred to him that she might be seeing another man somewhere, and he approached her nervously, but he was unprepared for the sudden anger he felt when he looked over her shoulder and saw that the letter was actually to Brent. "Please leave my son alone," he said carefully. He seemed to be losing control of his temper. He shouted at her in the kitchen, then walked into the living room where he noticed that nearly all of Abbie's things had been replaced, then wandered out onto the lawn. That afternoon he took her to a steak house on the shore in Plymouth, where he told her, gravely, that he felt things had gotten out of hand.

"I just wanted Brent to know I was there for him," she said apologetically.

But again Wilson lost his temper. He told her that Brent might very well be driven away by such demonstrations—although even as he said this he suspected it wasn't true—and ended by saying, so loud that the other diners turned toward them, "No, you're not. You are *not* there for my son."

She disappeared as abruptly as she had come. In a few days Wilson found it difficult to remember what they had even had together. Again he found himself aware of the emptiness of the house.

After that he discovered the bar scene. Each establishment attracted a certain category of woman, and it didn't take him long to learn the map. There was a place off Boston Common where the electronics industry gathered. The women here wore beige silk blouses, drank white wine, and spent a lot of time, Wilson thought, trying to look confident. They came in twos and paired off with the industry salesmen staying in the downtown hotels. Wilson decided it was a bad career move to spend time here. Further toward the river was a publishing hangout, where the women were younger and seemed more willing to converse. Wilson didn't know whether he was handsome, but he seemed to do all right with these types, and now and then he got a phone number. As often as not, though, the number was wrong. Sometimes he found himself fighting back discouragement. There was a bankers' bar and a travel-industry bar and a bar near Mass General for nurses, and over the months Wilson learned them all.

He made friends with a couple of local computer salesmen named Milos and Hank, and on any night he could call one of them to make the rounds with him. They were coarse people, and it was difficult at first, but then he learned to laugh at it. He tried not to think of Abbie. Milos drank doubles and used expressions like "beaver" and "monster truck," and Hank liked to say, "Bend over, I'll drive you to Cleveland." Instead of boasting, however, they traded stories about their most amusing failures. This surprised Wilson, but later he realized how well the tactic worked. Soon it became easy, and eventually fun. He developed a dialogue, spiced with self-deprecating humor, that caught women off-guard.

Later, though, if he saw these women again, he had to try to make the delicate transition away from what they might have thought he was in the bar. He was well aware that at Ned Clancy's only joking got their attention, but at dinner, or in one of the downtown cafes where he met the more cautious ones, the conversation had to have substance or it would flounder. Small talk became very serious. They discussed *goals* and *expectations*—words Wilson had never used until he found himself trying to seduce divorced women—and, for the ones who still seemed wounded, *loss* and *renewal.* He had never known so many people reassessing their lives. He dreaded the moment when he and a woman seemed to come to the end of their humor, because invariably the next step was to become overly thoughtful. Some sort of confession was required. Often, before dinner had even arrived, he found himself expounding about feelings he wasn't even sure he really had. The women he dated were close to his own age, but they seemed to have more in common with Brent.

The game would be starting momentarily, and as Wilson and Brent crossed the T tracks, pedestrians moving toward the park crowded the sidewalk. Wilson didn't recognize many faces; the regulars either arrived early to watch the hitters or not until the second inning. Fathers and sons were walking in pairs, but there were plenty of women, too, some of them alone. This always surprised him. The women he knew didn't go to ball games. He glanced about. There seemed to be something wrong with all the ones he could see; one who looked attractive turned out to be coarse-featured, another had the loose skin of a problem drinker, two were in Red Sox windbreakers. It pained him to look at the world like this, but then he thought of Milos and Hank, and he laughed. "Actually," he said, "it's seriously hard to meet them."

"It's what?" said Brent. They were near the stadium now, and the hurrying crowd was pushing through the haze of sausage smoke toward the gates.

"You asked if I was seeing anybody."

For a moment as they were pulled toward the gates he considered taking his son into his confidence, but the sudden proximity of so many people took away his courage. Abbie used to conduct their occasional serious dinner talks by announcing that Brent was not a child anymore, then asking him questions about drugs or venereal disease, and although this parental frankness used to bother Wilson, he had been wondering lately whether it might be a good idea. It was probably not right for a father to bother a son with his own problems, but he was well aware that their relationship had changed. Brent obviously did not think of Wilson as invulnerable anymore.

They reached their seats just as the Red Sox came to the plate, and Brent said, "Where are you looking?"

"All the wrong places, I guess."

"Are you going to bars?"

Wilson looked around. "Excuse me," he said, "I didn't know we were in court. Hey, Boggs is up."

"Boggs never swings at the first pitch," said Brent.

"Hey, they teach you that in Oregon?"

"No, you told me."

The Yankee pitcher went into his windup, threw a called strike, and against his will Wilson recalled that even Wade Boggs had been involved in a scandal with a woman. Boggs was the most methodical hitter in the majors, but for a while a few seasons back the scandal had affected his hitting. It involved a lawsuit, and his average had dipped. Sportswriters had used the opportunity to take jabs at him, and Wilson could remember thinking that what Boggs had done was despicable. But Boggs had struggled through it, and now Wilson realized he felt kinship with him, as if both of them had been wronged. Boggs tapped his cleats and singled into center field.

"Actually," Wilson said, "what's very hard is to meet a woman like your mother."

"I know, Dad."

"They don't exist anymore."

Brent was silent. There was a pop-up and two fly-outs, and the inning was over. As the Red Sox took the field Brent said, "Maybe you're looking in the wrong places, Dad, and maybe you're looking the wrong way, but they *do* exist."

Wilson thought about this while Clemens took his warm-ups. He couldn't remember the last time he had felt protective of Abbie. Finally, he said, "I hope your mother never hears you say that."

By the third, Wilson could see that Clemens was in for a hard day. He was throwing smoke but the ball was creeping out of the strike zone and the Yankee hitters were laying off. He walked a man in the first, got to three-and-one on a batter in the second, and stomped off the mound in the third after the umpire called a ball. Wilson booed.

"Who are you booing at?" Brent asked, "Clemens or the ump?"

"I just like to boo."

The stadium was erupting in catcalls and hisses; to their left, a kid in a B.U. sweatshirt stumbled down to the restraining fence alongside the bleachers, gave the finger to the umpire, and then threw his eyeglasses into the outfield. An old woman yelled, "Let the blind S.O.B. find 'em for you!"

The umpire called time out, and the Red Sox batboy ran into the field to pick up the glasses. He sprinted back along the foul line and as he turned into the dugout pretended to offer them to the umpire. The bleachers thundered.

"How could anyone see that pitch from here?" Brent said. Wilson chuckled. "Left-field telescopic vision, son."

"You know, you can see why there are wars in the world."

It was exactly the kind of overserious comment Brent had been making lately, and as he leaned back next to him in the sun, Wilson wondered what had happened to his son that hadn't happened to the other young men sitting around them. To his left, three guys in Zete T-shirts stood up, turned their backs to the plate, dropped their pants, waited for the bouncers to arrive, and then were escorted out of the stadium as a whole other section of Zetes stood up and cheered. Some of those Zetes had to have divorced parents.

"So, if you don't mind my asking," Wilson said, "What's the right way to look for girls?"

"Listen," said Brent.

Wilson looked at him, waiting for him to continue, but Brent had become absorbed in the game and Wilson suddenly realized that this was his answer, that you looked for girls by *listening* to them. He chuckled out loud. He himself had never said anything so self-righteous in his life, even as a college student, but in Oregon Brent and his friends had somehow learned to utter this kind of nonsense with conviction. Now Brent was watching the game with earnest composure. The Yankees sent a runner across and took the lead, and he leaned forward in his seat. There were two runners on base now, and every time Clemens threw a pitch, Brent's right arm tensed. It was hard to figure him out.

"I was under the impression you guys didn't do that," Wilson said.

"Do what?"

"You know, make time with the ladies."

Brent didn't look up from the field. "Sure we do, just not the way you do. We're honest about it."

Wilson turned back to the game. Brent was annoying him, actually. Wilson had the crazy urge to tell him that his old man had in fact developed quite a skill at working the downtown bars, that it was not so easy proffering conversation to educated women in silk blouses. He imagined Brent trying it. He imagined Brent calling a wrong number that had been scrawled on a cocktail napkin. He wanted to tell him about the stewardess in Washington and about going to bed with a woman he had hit in an intersection, but Clemens managed to put down the side, and as the Red Sox ran in from their positions Wilson was overtaken by shame instead. What in God's name had happened to him? He realized how much he would miss Brent tomorrow. He had taken him to his first game when he was barely two months old, wrapping him in a red-and-blue blanket that Abbie had made and holding him aloft under the night lights. Brent had been captivated by their glare. Abbie was worried about the chilly evening, but those were the old days and she had gone along, and after all the young wives cooed at Brent, she had gone home proud. From then on they went to a dozen games a year. Wilson had wanted his son to love baseball. He had wanted to share with him the beauty of the great, green, breathtaking panorama in front of them.

Clemens calmed down in the fourth and began to overpower the Yankees, but by the sixth he had started to tire, and in the seventh he came out of the game, kicking the rosin bag in the air. The Red Sox led, 2–1, but two walked Yankees were on base and Mattingly was coming to the plate. The crowd booed absently. Wilson overheard the usher talking about The Curse. Reardon came in and walked two batters. By the time Wilson and Brent were waiting in line for hot dogs at the inning break, the Yankees led, 5–2.

Inside, the concession line wound back through the dark corridor and was filled with grumbling fans. To Wilson, some of them looked truly stricken, and he wondered at their foolhardiness. "Of course the Sox are going to blow it," he said to a man next to them. "They're the Sox."

Nonetheless, inside the stadium Wilson had felt disappointed and chilled. It would have been nice for Brent to see a victory. A few places in front of them in line a fat man gave off the odor of booze so sharply that Wilson wondered if he too ever smelled like that after the one or two glasses of wine he usually had at dinner or the scotches he drank in the bars. Brent noticed it also. Wilson could see him watching, looking the man up and down with the strange type of distaste he'd noticed in young people lately. It was an odd prudishness, and Brent seemed to feel it deeply. When the man moved forward in line he took deliberate, stiff steps, trying to act sober, and Brent turned away.

"Say," said Wilson, "you going to stop by The Sanctuary while you're here?"

"Right," Brent said. "Maybe say hi to the gals."

Wilson laughed. It was a relief to hear a joke about it finally. "Whoa," he whispered quickly, "mermaid on the rocks."

"What?"

It was a gag that Milos and Hank used in the bars, but it had slipped out. He shifted his eyes behind Brent, toward a well-dressed woman who had just taken her place next to them in line, and whispered, "What do you say, captain?"

Brent looked around.

"Beaver in the water," Wilson finally said, lowering his voice even further. Even as he said this he felt sick, but it had come out now, and suddenly he felt that as long as it was the truth, it was all right for Brent to hear it. He turned his back to the woman and winked.

Brent smiled thinly. Wilson was feeling almost giddy. He winked again and whispered, "Ready the nets."

Brent thought for a moment. "Do you ever talk to Mom?" he said loudly.

There was nothing Wilson could say. When he glanced behind him the woman was looking at the ceiling, and he wondered whether she'd heard their whole conversation. God, how had he gotten to where he was? When Brent was in junior high, Wilson and Abbie used to chaperone the school dances, and at the end of high school, when Brent began dating girls, Wilson had taught him to always go inside his date's house to meet the parents.

"I'm afraid we haven't talked in quite some time," he said. Then he shouted, "Polish, Polish, chips, chips, Bud, Coke," to his friend Maurice, the hot-dog vendor, and moved in quickly to the counter. *Albany, Atlanta, Augusta,* he repeated to himself. Knots of men clustered around him at the mustard tubs, slathering sauerkraut on hot dogs and cursing the Red Sox. *Austin, Baton Rouge, Bismarck.* He was used to shame from his evenings out with Milos and Hank, to waking up and recalling their sarcastic renditions of failure in the back booth at Ned Clancy's, but now he had demeaned himself in front of his own son.

He shouted his order again, and Maurice shouted back, "He's stinking today," which took Wilson several moments to understand.

As Maurice gave him the sausages Wilson muttered back, "Can't buy a strike." Then he said, "Maurice, this is my son, Brent. Brent loves your sausages." He gestured to his side, but when he turned around Brent was gone.

"Handsome kid," said Maurice.

Wilson shrugged and moved away toward the mustard tubs. He didn't want to look around, in case Brent was watching. He loaded up the sausages, layering Brent's with sauerkraut and ketchup the way he used to like them, and rewrapped them carefully in the wax paper.

When he looked up it took him several moments to find Brent, because he was standing with the woman who had been next to them in line. They were behind a column, shielding themselves from the streaming crowd, and they were talking. Wilson had the sudden thought that his son was apologizing for him, and he told himself that he didn't care. As far as he was concerned, Brent could do what he damn well pleased. Then he stepped over and saw that the woman was doing the talking and that Brent was mostly just nodding his head and pursing his lips in his familiar way.

He mustered up a jovial voice. "Hello, there," he said, stepping forward. "I'm Wilson, and I'll be your waiter."

The woman laughed. "Waiter," she said, "this soup is cold." Then she laughed again, closing her eyes.

"Dad," Brent said, "this is Margaret. Margaret, this is my father, Wilson."

Wilson didn't know what to say, and in a moment Brent was speaking again, asking her something as they started down the dark corridor. Her seat was behind home plate, it turned out, and she and Brent continued their conversation as they walked. Wilson fell behind in the crowd, guarding the sausages. The corridor brightened and darkened. He could tell Milos and Hank about this on Thursday, at the Dunked Rose. "My own son," he would say, affecting a hangdog look. "My twenty-year-old son."

When he got back to the seats, he handed Brent a sausage and said, "Not bad for a rookie."

"Ditto for an old-timer," said Brent.

Wilson laughed. "But a sale's not a sale if you don't close, buckaroo."

"You know, Dad, you should see someone like Margaret. I liked her a lot."

"Thanks, kid," Wilson said, "but I do fine on my own."

In the eighth, with nobody out and Red Sox on first and third, Wilson started to hope. They were still trailing by three, and he knew better, but nonetheless he felt the rise in his blood. The first out came on a called strike. "Don't blow it," he said. He leaned forward in his seat, and when a wave came through their section, he leapt up. The count went to three-and-two. Then came an infield pop-up, and the crowd booed. A section of Yankee fans began to cheer and thump their seats. "Watch this," Wilson said, "they're going to blow it," and on the next pitch Gatling hit a weak fly to right and the inning was over. "Damn it," he said. "Damn it, damn it."

"It's only a game, Dad."

The Red Sox would always do this, but even after all these years he felt the disappointment each time. No matter who they picked up in trades, no matter who they paid five million dollars for, they were doomed to lose. He sat low in his seat. Coming onto the field now was a team he barely knew. The old team of 1986, the team that had almost done it, was gone. They were the ones who had truly broken his heart. They'd come one out away from the world championship and then, crazily, catastrophically, given the game to the Mets. That team was broken up now. Marty Barrett was gone, Tony Armas was gone, poor Bill Buckner was gone. Bill Buckner was the truest Red Sock, snake-bit, the man who played the Series with taped ankles and high-top cleats, grimacing in pain, only to muff the ninth-inning grounder that would have won it all for Boston.

"Hey," Wilson said to Brent, "Did you hear that Bill Buckner tried to commit suicide?"

"Poor man," Brent answered. "You mean after the Series? There was a lot of pressure on him."

"Yeah," Wilson said, "he jumped in front of a subway train." He tried to look serious. "But it went through his legs."

Brent was nodding, the way he had to Margaret.

"That's a joke," Wilson said. "The train went through his legs."

"Why don't you see somebody?" Brent said.

"Hey, slugger, I do."

"I mean a therapist or somebody."

"That stuff's not for me."

"I'm not saying there's anything wrong," Brent said. "I'm just saying you seem sad."

"I *am* sad," Wilson said. "I'm sad that the Sox can't score a run. I'm also sad that you think I need to see a therapist."

Brent finished his sausage, folded up the wrapper, and set it underneath his seat. "Mom sees one," he said.

"How do you know that?"

"We talk about it."

"Well, then, maybe he'll tell her why she left us."

"Maybe *she'll* tell her, you mean," Brent said, "but I doubt it. That's not what therapists do." This was his only answer. He leaned back in his seat and put his arm over Wilson's shoulder, and he kept it there for the rest of the inning. Wilson was angry but grateful. The Yankees went down in order. He didn't feel like talking, and they watched the game in silence. At one point he actually imagined Billy Buckner walking down to the Fenway T stop and jumping onto the tracks.

As the Red Sox came to the plate in the bottom of the ninth, Brent said, "I asked Margaret to come to dinner with us."

* * *

The Red Sox lost, and after the game Wilson brought Brent home and showed him the house. He hadn't seen it since Easter, and Wilson couldn't help showing him several things Brent probably thought were ridiculous—the new garbage disposal he'd had installed, a row of bricks he'd replaced himself along the garden walk—even though he was struck by how similar this was to what Brent used to do, as a child, when Wilson and Abbie visited his bunk on the last day of overnight camp. Wilson was aware of his time running out. Brent nodded and followed him around the house. Then, just before they left for dinner, Brent went upstairs to make a phone call, and when he came down he said, "Good, she's meeting us there."

"You're kidding," Wilson said, "Right? Tell me you're kidding."

"No joke, Dad."

"You talked to the dame for five minutes at the ballpark, and now she's joining us for dinner?"

"We talked for longer than five minutes."

"Okay, ten minutes."

"Yeah, well, we connected. I listened to her."

Wilson didn't want to answer this. He felt the mixture of bafflement and ire that he knew from their brunches at the Charles Hotel. Was Brent implying that Wilson himself didn't listen? If only Brent knew how much he wanted to hear everything about him, to be a part of the strange, distant life that his son had come to lead. Again he fought back discouragement. In the car on the way into Cambridge he talked about the game instead, because he didn't want to mar their last few hours together. He had brought this on himself, he knew, with the borrowed antics of Milos and Hank. He glanced at his watch.

He talked absently about the final innings, and as they were parking he said, "So, let me get this straight, you use this listening business to make time with dames?"

"I don't use it for anything, I just do it."

"But you were able to get this dame to dinner."

"I invited her to dinner because I liked her. We had a wonderful conversation."

"About what? Does she like mustard?"

"We talked about serious things."

"Ah," Wilson said, "the Oregon maneuver."

"Her father has cancer. That's one thing."

"Oh, God," Wilson said. "I didn't mean to joke."

"It's okay, she's used to it."

"To the cancer, you mean."

"Right."

"Not to me joking."

"Not to you joking," said Brent.

As they made their way up the sidewalk Wilson watched him. He even walked in a serious way, his arms pulled in tight to his sides, his hands in his pockets. Actually, it was impressive, Wilson had to admit—the way he moved among women, the way he seemed to be privy to their secret communication. Maybe it was his seriousness, after all; maybe it reassured them. Maybe this was why he had been allowed to work at The Sanctuary.

As they neared the restaurant Margaret stepped from a taxi, and Brent hurried ahead to greet her. Wilson watched them. Brent held the door for her, which was interesting because Wilson was under the impression the younger generation didn't do this for a lady anymore. Wilson fixed his tie. The whole thing was ridiculous. In the dimmed light Margaret seemed to be in her early fifties, and as they passed through the atrium into the dining room Brent actually touched her, lightly, on the small of her back, and guided her. It was an old-world gesture.

Now Brent had pulled out her chair for her, and Wilson realized he was being a little slow. It was ridiculous, but for a moment as he struggled to cross the restaurant and catch up with them it occurred to him that his son was trying to show him how to put the moves on a woman his mother's age. Wilson had the sudden, piercing memory of opening the bathroom door one Sunday afternoon years ago and surprising Brent's high school girlfriend, Marjorie, as she stepped from the shower. She had paused with the curtain open, and Wilson—although he really hadn't meant to—had paused as well, before he apologized and shut the door. He had never told Brent about it, but it struck him now, strangely, that perhaps *she* had told him instead. He stepped quickly toward the table. Brent said something to Margaret that made her laugh, and Wilson took his seat between them.

The dinner was well prepared—it always was—but Wilson felt disoriented watching the two of them, listening to them as though they were speaking in another room and he was hearing them through a wall. He leaned forward and tried to concentrate. They were talking about politics, of course, but Wilson couldn't help being impressed with Brent's conversational ingenuity. Instead of carping about the administration, as Wilson was tempted to do, Brent was trying to discern her opinions. He asked what she had thought about the different presidential candidates, about the glass ceiling in corporate America, and about the climate surrounding women in professional positions. Margaret talked enthusiastically. Wilson couldn't decide whether to be dismayed or buoyed. Had men of his son's generation merely taken a different tack—and perhaps a better one—to the same old goal of finding, attracting, and seducing a woman? Or had they somehow taken on the cause of women as their own? As for himself, he couldn't talk about these things. It wouldn't sit right.

During dinner Margaret made it a point to ask Wilson a number of questions—she was graceful socially—but even as he answered he was aware of faint amusement on Brent's part. Several times, he could not think of how to keep the conversation moving. At one point, after going on too long, he found himself launching into a presentation on Japanese microchips that he had memorized for a marketing meeting that week. Brent smiled, and after a pause he asked Margaret what she had thought of the Hill-Thomas hearings.

Wilson ordered another glass of wine. It was definitely ridiculous. What was Brent trying to do? His plane was leaving for the West Coast in two hours. If he was trying to show Wilson that he knew how to handle himself with a woman, he was going too far. And if he was actually trying to teach Wilson something—well, he had a thing or two coming. Brent wouldn't last an evening in the downtown bars. Didn't Margaret know this? He looked over at her. She was saying something about the secretary of labor, and Brent was nodding again. He seemed to be gazing at her.

Finally, between dinner and desert, Brent excused himself to use the bathroom, and when he was gone Wilson sipped his wine and looked over the glass at Margaret.

"Your son is charming," she said.

He took another sip of wine and set down the glass. "He's a youngster," he said. He tore off a piece of bread. Then he added, "He's a good kid."

"He's so concerned."

This seemed to be a good sign, and Wilson laughed. "God knows where he gets that from."

She looked thoughtful. "He gets it from you, I think. He reminds me of my own son. After my husband and I were divorced, Michael went to work on an Indian reservation."

"Is that right? Brent used to work at a women's shelter."

"Which one?"

"A place called The Sanctuary."

"In Porter Square," she said.

Wilson sipped his wine. "I don't know where it is, actually," he said. "He wouldn't ever tell me. He told me it was a secret he promised to keep."

"Good for him for keeping it, then. I probably shouldn't have told you either."

"I can't wait to tell the guys at Ned Clancy's."

She smirked.

"Just kidding," said Wilson.

"Brent said you were one of the most serious people he knew."

"He said that about *me?*"

"Sure did."

"Poor kid," said Wilson. "He doesn't know many people."

Margaret laughed, and Wilson paused, enjoying the audience. Then he said, "Excuse me, I forgot to ask about your children."

"Two sons," she said. Then she added softly, "Grown now."

She sipped her wine, and Wilson was suddenly aware what it meant for her to say this. His glance fell to her hands. "Do you miss them?" he asked.

"Terribly," she said.

"I do too," said Wilson, and then, crazily, he wanted to take her hand. He took another sip of wine and waited without speaking for several moments, watching her fingers.

"You know what I like about you?" he said finally.

"Tell me."

"That Brent likes you."

"Funny," she answered, "that's what I like about *you*."

After dinner they put Margaret in a cab, and Wilson made the drive with Brent out to Logan. Rain had begun to fall, and as he sluiced the Lincoln through the puddles, he felt an unfamiliar ease between the two of them. He didn't know if it was coming from him or from Brent, but on the short section of highway Brent let him rest his hand on his shoulder, and at the terminal he waited in the car a few moments before he got out to retrieve his luggage from the trunk. Wilson walked him to the gate.

"Hey, slugger," he said, when it was time to board, "how many mice does it take to screw in a light bulb?"

"Two," Brent answered, "but they have to be small. That's prehistoric."

"I know," Wilson said, "but I just got it a couple of days ago."

"Don't sweat it, Dad."

"Hey, it was good to have you out here, kid."

"It was good to be here, kid," Brent said. Then he reached over and kissed Wilson on the cheek. "By the way," he said as he turned, "I like Margaret."

"So do I," said Wilson, and then Brent went through the gate.

It was remarkable how easily he and Margaret grew together. That week he took her to dinner, where they talked about Brent and her own children, and afterward they walked down to the esplanade and sat on the benches by the Charles. Even then, the first time they had ever been alone together, he had the feeling of having known her for a long time, and he hoped for some small crisis—a car accident or a lost dog—that would prove their ease with each other. Driving her home, he took a detour through the dark, forested neighborhoods of Brookline and drove by Brent's junior high school, where they stopped to watch the moonlight playing over the great trees on the lawn. She said, "He must have been a very sweet child," and Wilson answered, "He was."

They had dinner again two nights later, and Wilson found himself talking about the smallest details of his life—how the cleaners that week had broken two buttons on one of his shirts, how much he liked his new showerhead—but rather than feeling desperate at this turn in the conversation, as he might have with one of the women from the bars, he felt elated. *These* were his secrets, and at last he was telling them. Later on, he thought to himself, they could talk about *goals* and *expectations,* in bed looking at the ceiling. He kissed her good night but that was all. He knew enough to go slow.

The next week, Margaret called him and told him what he pretended not to already know, that her father was sick, and then she broke into tears and said that he had taken a turn for the worse. She wept openly on the phone, and he knew they were at a crossroads. He was hesitant to ask about the cancer; Brent had asked about it in a hot dog line at Fenway, but this was the protocol of a different generation, and instead Wilson just let her talk. He hoped she would stop sobbing between sentences, and she did eventually, after which there was a silence. It went on for several moments, and then he offered to go with her to visit.

Two days later they were together on a plane to Rochester,

Minnesota, where the old man was in the hospital. Ordinarily, the way he did with business trips, Wilson would have telephoned Brent with his itinerary—even though Brent laughed at these precautions—but this time Wilson could not bring himself to do it. He left a message on his own answering machine instead, assuming Brent wouldn't call. Then they left. To avoid any problems, Wilson booked them into separate rooms at the hotel, and that afternoon they went to see her father. Wilson was nervous. He didn't know how to explain his own presence, either to himself or to the old man, and as he waited in line in the lobby florist shop he rehearsed various things he might say to him. But when they entered the hospital room the poor old man was vomiting in the side-sink, and Margaret took his hand. Wilson took Margaret's, and at that moment he realized he might be falling in love.

It was not the way he had expected it. The room stunk of floor cleaner and medicines, and the half-comatose old man in the room's other bed was opening and closing his mouth like a fish. Margaret did not look particularly beautiful—it was not *that*—but she looked determined and kind, and when she rubbed the mottled back of her father's hand, Wilson understood what her presence would have meant to him if he himself had been dying. Was this the way a middle-aged man fell in love?

By the time her father had quieted down and Margaret had wiped him off, the feeling was gone, and Wilson was relieved. But that evening going down in the hospital elevator, Margaret distractedly pulled his jacket straight and he felt the same thing again for a moment—a great, familiar comfort that made him take her face in his hands and kiss her, right there in the elevator. It occurred to him how much time he had wasted in bars. Then they were in the bright, fluorescent lobby with its silk plants and antiseptic residue, and the feeling was gone again. But this was the way it started, he knew, stuttering like this, and he had not felt it in a long time.

That night he moved his bags to her hotel room and they slept there together, but he did not want to make love to her under the circumstances. He held her as though he might have been holding his wife of thirty years, and they went to sleep without speaking. Comfort seemed to be something they had both learned in their marriages, although when he woke early the next morning and wondered momentarily where he was— the hotel shook with the sound of descending airplanes—his heart sank at how easily his own allegiance had been transferred. He fought for courage.

But this was how his future was going to unfold, he came to accept, by such a strange bit of chance. His son had introduced him to a woman at a baseball game, and now she was flying home with him, sleeping on his shoulder in the airplane. Less than a week later they were in Minnesota again at her father's funeral, and in October they drove up to New Hampshire to visit her in-laws.

Wilson wrote a letter.

Dear Buckaroo—

Although I suspect this to be of little interest to you, I will report on the Red Sox. There are only a few games remaining and I am sad to say that Boston stands twenty-three games out of first place, which is a disappointment to all of us although tempered by the fact that New York stands out twenty. Wait till next year!

I wanted to tell you that your friend Margaret and I have been seeing each other. You were right. She's wonderful, smart like your mother and almost as beautiful. Maybe she'll be here for Thanksgiving when you come.

I also wanted to tell you that her father passed away last

week, which I know you will be sorry to hear. From what she told me, it was a good thing for all concerned, so you needn't be unduly upset. Margaret is handling it well.

What's new in the girl department for you, by the way? Seeing anybody? How are your classes?

I know writing is a burden, so call me collect when you feel like it.

How does a blonde turn on the light after sex?

I love you and always will,
Wilson

(She opens the car door.)

Brent didn't write back, but he phoned a week later, full of questions about Margaret. What had they done together? How often was he seeing her? Wilson was hesitant at first, because in the letter he hadn't mentioned going to Minnesota, but there seemed to be enthusiasm in Brent's voice, and he discovered he was happy to talk about her. He was surprised at the relief he felt when Brent did not seem hurt, and his mood became garrulous. He told Brent about walking down to the Charles on their first evening together and feeling the kind of comfort he had not felt since Abbie had left. But suddenly, after he said this, he was afraid he had transgressed. He asked Brent whether he needed money to fly home for Thanksgiving, but Brent came right back to the subject of Margaret. Was she upset about her father, he wanted to know. At this point Wilson slipped in that they had gone to Minnesota together, and for a moment there seemed to be a pause on Brent's end of the line. Then he resumed saying "uh-huh" every few seconds, and Wilson could picture him nodding on the other end. Before they hung up, Brent asked for her address.

The next day Wilson found himself thinking about her at

work. He wondered what Brent would write in a letter to her, and whether she would answer in the confidential, serious way they had talked at dinner. It was a comforting thought, somehow, that his son had secrets with her, even though this was the very thing that had caused him to lose his temper with Mary-Jane Donnelly. He didn't understand. His own heart sometimes seemed like something he could look at only from a distance, like some small animal in a cage.

In the early afternoon he called Panos the florist and told him he wanted to send roses to Margaret's house. Panos whispered, *discreet, discreet,* into the phone, and Wilson laughed. Then he realized that he hadn't bought flowers since Abbie had left and that Panos probably thought he was still married. He started to explain but was overtaken by a shuddering sadness. Panos laughed, a low chuckle, saying *no need, my friend,* and asked Wilson what he wanted on the card. There was a silence before the florist suggested, *From an admirer,* and Wilson, fighting to steady his voice, agreed.

He hadn't been ready for such a collapse. There seemed to be a part of him that he no longer controlled, a ruinous version of himself that brought up memories of his old life as soon as he was ready to embark on a new one. It had been years since Abbie had cared what he did, but even now he couldn't help thinking that he was crossing her. He called Panos again and doubled the order of roses, and before he met Margaret that night for dinner, he drank two scotches in a bar on Mass Avenue and went for a walk along the river. Whenever Abbie came to mind he went through the state capitals, and when that didn't work he made an attempt to recall the organizational structure of the 486 microchip. He told himself that melancholy was natural under the circumstances, but suddenly, crossing under a footbridge, he had trouble remembering the woman he was about to see. He couldn't recall what her voice was like or how she looked, and when he entered the restaurant a few minutes later he went to the men's room and examined himself in the mirror because he was afraid his feelings would show on his face. Then he was afraid that Margaret had made the same sort of reappraisal of him. But when he got to the table she was already there, and when she stood and kissed him he remembered the roses and realized his fears were unfounded. By the time dinner was over he couldn't exactly remember what he had been afraid of.

Two nights later, crossing the Mass Avenue Bridge in a rainstorm, Wilson first thought about marrying Margaret. He pulled over past the bridge, got his breath, and continued toward home. Rain thrummed on the roof of the car. He passed MIT, then Central Square, then the edge of his own neighborhood where he saw Panos emerge into the rain to throw a bag in the garbage, and just as suddenly, as the old florist hobbled back into his shop, he realized it might not be love he was feeling with Margaret, but merely the reconstruction of his memory of love. Tears sprang to his eyes. How simple he seemed to himself, like a schoolgirl overcome by familiarity. It was the first time since Abbie had left that he had shared Brent with a woman; this was all that had happened. Houses flashed by.

He continued up Mass Avenue in the rain. Ahead of him in a station wagon a little boy was making faces at the other drivers, and suddenly, as he swept down into the cool darkness of the Cambridge Street tunnel, a thought occurred to him: that Brent was never again going to spend a summer at home, and that this was why he had set him up with Margaret. It was a condolence.

He turned left off Cambridge Avenue and reached Porter Square in a few minutes, where he pulled over and stopped the car, his breath shallow with grief. The rain was steady and the neon lights were twisted in the windshield. The doorways were dark. A woman passed quickly up the sidewalk under an umbrella, but she kept walking, beyond the end of the square and back into the darkness. He sat low. There were as many worlds of anguish as there were doors, it seemed to him, or porches, or chimneys. He didn't know if he would recognize a women's shelter if he saw one, but he waited there anyway, because he wanted to feel, if only distantly and for a moment, what his son had felt. When he became drowsy he opened the window and held his face up to the rain. Cars moved by; lights went on and off; shades were lowered. Brent was gone now, he was thinking, off to make his own, unimaginable way in the world.

IV

▲

THE PALACE THIEF

I tell this story not for my own honor, for there is little of that here, and not as a warning, for a man of my calling learns quickly that all warnings are in vain. Nor do I tell it in apology for St. Benedict's School, for St. Benedict's School needs no apologies. I tell it only to record certain foretellable incidents in the life of a well-known man, in the event that the brief candle of his days may sometime come under the scrutiny of another student of history. That is all. This is a story without surprises.

There are those, in fact, who say I should have known what would happen between St. Benedict's and me, and I suppose that they are right; but I loved that school. I gave service there to the minds of three generations of boys and always left upon them, if I was successful, the delicate imprint of their culture. I battled their indolence with discipline, their boorishness with philosophy, and the arrogance of their stations with the history of great men before them. I taught the sons of nineteen senators. I taught a boy who, if not for the vengeful recriminations of the tabloids, would today have been president of the United States. That school was my life.

This is why, I suppose, I accepted the invitation sent to me by Mr. Sedgewick Bell at the end of last year, although I should have known better. I suppose I should have recalled what kind of boy he had been at St. Benedict's forty-one years before instead of posting my response so promptly in the mail and beginning that evening to prepare my test. He, of course, was the son of Senator Sedgewick Hyram Bell, the West Virginia demagogue who kept horses at his residence in Washington, D.C., and had swung several southern states for Wendell Wilkie. The younger Sedgewick was a dull boy.

I first met him when I had been teaching history at St. Benedict's for only five years, in the autumn after his father had been delivered to office on the shoulders of southern patricians frightened by the unionization of steel and mine workers. Sedgewick appeared in my classroom in November of 1945, in a short-pants suit. It was midway through the fall term, that term in which I brought the boys forth from the philosophical idealism of the Greeks into the realm of commerce, military might, and the law, which had given Julius Caesar his prerogative from Macedonia to Seville. My students, of course, were agitated. It is a sad distinction of that age group, the exuberance with which the boys abandon the moral endeavor of Plato and embrace the powerful, pragmatic hand of Augustus. The more sensitive ones had grown silent, and for several weeks our class discussions had been dominated by the martial instincts of the coarser boys. Of course I was sorry for this, but I was well aware of the import of what I taught at St. Benedict's. Our headmaster, Mr. Woodbridge, made us continually aware of the role our students would eventually play in the affairs of our country.

My classroom was in fact a tribute to the lofty ideals of man, which I hoped would inspire my boys, and at the same time to the fleeting nature of human accomplishment, which I hoped would temper their ambition with humility. It was a dual tactic, with which Mr. Woodbridge heartily agreed. Above the door frame hung a tablet, made as a term project by Henry L. Stimson when he was a boy here, that I hoped would teach my students of the irony that history bestows upon ambition. In clay relief it said:

> I am Shutruk-Nahhunte, King of Anshan and Susa,
>   sovereign of the land of Elam.
> By the command of Inshushinak,
> I destroyed Sippar, took the stele of Naram-Sin,
>   and brought it back to Elam,
> where I erected it as an offering to my god,
>   Inshushinak.
>
> —Shutruk-Nahhunte, 1158 B.C.

I always noted this tablet to the boys on their first day in my classroom, partly to inform them of their predecessors at St. Benedict's and partly to remind them of the great ambition and conquest that had been utterly forgotten centuries before they were born. Afterward I had one of them recite, from the wall where it hung above my desk, Shelley's "Ozymandias." It is critical for any man of import to understand his own insignificance before the sands of time, and this is what my classroom always showed my boys.

As young Sedgewick Bell stood in the doorway of that classroom his first day at St. Benedict's, however, it was apparent that such efforts would be lost on him. I could see that he was not only a dullard but a roustabout. The boys happened to be wearing the togas they had made from sheets and safety pins the day before, spreading their knees like magistrates in the wooden desk chairs, and I was taking them through the recitation of the emperors, when Mr. Woodbridge entered alongside the stout, red-faced Sedgewick, and introduced him to the class.

I had taught for several years already, as I have said, and I knew the look of frightened, desperate bravura on a new boy's face. Sedgewick Bell did not wear this look. Rather, he wore one of disdain. The boys, fifteen in all, were instantly intimidated into sensing the foolishness of their improvised cloaks, and one of them, Fred Masoudi, the leader of the dullards— though far from a dullard himself—said, to mild laughter, "Where's your toga, kid?"

Sedgewick Bell answered, "Your mother must be wearing your pants today."

It took me a moment to regain the attention of the class, and when Sedgewick was seated I had him go to the board and copy out the emperors. Of course, he did not know the names of any of them, and my boys had to call them out, repeatedly correcting his spelling as he wrote out in a sloppy hand:

Augustus
Tiberius
Caligula
Claudius
Nero
Galba
Otho

all the while lifting and resettling the legs of his short pants in mockery of what his new classmates were wearing. "Young man," I said, "this is a serious class, and I expect that you will take it seriously."

"If it's such a serious class, then why're they all wearing dresses?" he responded, again to laughter, although by now

Fred Masoudi had loosened the rope belt at his waist and the boys around him were shifting uncomfortably in their togas.

From that first day, Sedgewick Bell was a boor and a bully, a damper to the illumination of the eager minds of my boys and a purveyor of the mean-spirited humor that is like kerosene in a school such as ours. What I asked of my boys that semester was simple—that they learn the facts I presented to them in an "Outline of Ancient Roman History," which I had whittled, through my years of teaching, to exactly four closely typed pages; yet Sedgewick Bell was unwilling to do so. He was a poor student and on his first exam could not even tell me who it was that Mark Antony and Octavian had routed at Philippi, nor who Octavian later became, although an average wood-beetle in the floor of my classroom could have done so with ease.

Furthermore, as soon as he arrived he began a stream of capers using spitballs, wads of gum, and thumbtacks. Of course it was common for a new boy to engage his comrades thusly, but Sedgewick Bell then began to add the dangerous element of natural leadership—which was based on the physical strength of his features—to his otherwise puerile antics. He organized the boys. At exactly fifteen minutes to the hour, they would all drop their pencils at once, or cough, or slap closed their books so that writing at the blackboard my hands would jump in the air.

At a boys' school, of course, punishment is a cultivated art. Whenever one of these antics occurred, I simply made a point of calling on Sedgewick Bell to answer a question. General laughter usually followed his stabs at answers, and although Sedgewick himself usually laughed along with everyone else, it did not require a great deal of insight to know that the tactic would work. The organized events began to occur less frequently.

In retrospect, however, perhaps my strategy was a mistake, for to convince a boy of his own stupidity is to shoot a poisonous arrow indeed. Perhaps Sedgewick Bell's life would have turned out more nobly if I had understood his motivations right away and treated him differently at the start. But such are the pointless speculations of a teacher. What was irrefutably true was that he was performing poorly on his quizzes, even if his behavior had improved somewhat, and therefore I called him to my office.

In those days I lived in small quarters off the rear of the main hall, in what had been a slave's room when the grounds of St. Benedict's had been the estate of the philanthropist and horse breeder Cyrus Beck. Having been at school as long as I had, I no longer lived in the first-form dormitory that stood behind my room, but supervised it, so that I saw most of the boys only in matters of urgency. They came sheepishly before me.

With my bed folded into the wall, the room became my office, and shortly after supper one day that winter of his first-form year, Sedgewick Bell knocked and entered. Immediately he began to inspect the premises, casting his eyes, which had the patrician set of his father's, from the desk to the shelves to the bed folded into the wall.

"Sit down, boy."

"You're not married, are you, sir?"

"No, Sedgewick, I am not. However, we are here to talk about *you*."

"That's why you like puttin' us in togas, right?"

Frankly, I had never encountered a boy like him before, who at the age of thirteen would affront his schoolmaster without other boys in audience. He gazed at me flatly, his chin in his hand.

"Young man," I said, sensing his motivations with sudden

clarity, "we are concerned about your performance here, and I have made an appointment to see your father."

In fact, I had made no appointment with Senator Bell, but at that moment I understood that I would have to. "What would you like me to tell the senator?" I said.

His gaze faltered. "I'm going to try harder, sir, from now on."

"Good, Sedgewick. Good."

Indeed, that week the boys reenacted the pivotal scenes from *Julius Caesar,* and Sedgewick read his lines quite passably and contributed little that I could see to the occasional fits of giggles that circulated among the slower boys. The next week, I gave a quiz on the triumvirate of Crassus, Pompey, and Caesar, and he passed for the first time yet, with a C plus.

Nonetheless, I had told him that I was going to speak with his father, and this is what I was determined to do. At the time, Senator Sedgewick Hyram Bell was appearing regularly in the newspapers and on the radio in his stand against Truman's plan for national health insurance, and I was loath to call upon such a well-known man concerning the behavior of his son. On the radio his voice was a tobacco drawl that had won him populist appeal throughout West Virginia, although his policies alone would certainly not have done so. I was at the time in my late twenties, and although I was armed with scruples and an education, my hands trembled as I dialed his office. To my surprise, I was put through, and the senator, in the drawl I recognized instantly, agreed to meet me one afternoon the following week. The man already enjoyed national stature, of course, and although any other father would no doubt have made the journey to St. Benedict's himself, I admit that the prospect of seeing the man in his own office intrigued me. Thus I journeyed to the capital.

St. Benedict's lies in the bucolic, equine expanse of rural Virginia, nearer in spirit to the Carolinas than to Maryland, although the drive to Washington requires little more than an hour. The bus followed the misty, serpentine course of the Passamic, then entered the marshlands that are now the false-brick suburbs of Washington, and at last left me downtown in the capital, where I proceeded the rest of the way on foot. I arrived at the Senate office building as the sun moved low against the bare-limbed cherries among the grounds. I was frightened but determined, and I reminded myself that Sedgewick Hyram Bell was a senator but also a father, and I was here on business that concerned his son. The office was as grand as a duke's.

I had not waited long in the anteroom when the man himself appeared, feisty as a game hen, bursting through a side door and clapping me on the shoulder as he urged me before him into his office. Of course I was a novice then in the world of politics and had not yet realized that such men are, above all, likeable. He put me in a leather seat, offered me a cigar, which I refused, and then with real or contrived wonder—perhaps he did something like this with all of his visitors—he proceeded to show me an antique sidearm that had been sent to him that morning by a constituent and that had once belonged, he said, to the coachman of Robert E. Lee. "You're a history buff," he said, "right?"

"Yes, sir."

"Then take it. It's yours."

"No, sir. I couldn't."

"Take the damn thing."

"All right, I will."

"Now, what brings you to this dreary little office?"

"Your son, sir."

"What the devil has he done now?"

"Very little, sir. We're concerned that he isn't learning the material."

"What material is that?"

"We're studying the Romans now, sir. We've left the Republic and entered the Empire."

"Ah," he said. "Be careful with that, by the way. It still fires."

"Your son seems not to be paying attention, sir."

He again offered me the box of cigars across the desk and then bit off the end of his own. "Tell me," he said, puffing the thing until it flamed suddenly, "What's the good of what you're teaching them boys?"

This was a question for which I was well prepared, fortunately, having recently written a short piece in *The St. Benedict's Crier* answering the same challenge put forth there by an anonymous boy. "When they read of the reign of Augustus Caesar," I said without hesitation, "when they learn that his rule was bolstered by commerce, a postal system, and the arts, by the reformation of the senate and by the righting of an inequitable system of taxation, when they see the effect of scientific progress through the census and the enviable network of Roman roads, how these advances led mankind away from the brutish rivalries of potentates into the two centuries of Pax Romana, then they understand the importance of character and high ideals."

He puffed at his cigar. "Now, that's a horse who can talk," he said. "And you're telling me my son Sedgewick has his head in the clouds."

"It's my job, sir, to mold your son's character."

He thought for a moment, idly fingering a match. Then his look turned stern. "I'm sorry, young man," he said slowly, "but you will not mold him. I will mold him. You will merely teach him."

That was the end of my interview, and I was politely shown the door. I was bewildered, naturally, and found myself in the elevator before I could even take account of what had happened. Senator Bell was quite likeable, as I have noted, but he had without doubt cut me, and as I made my way back to the bus station, the gun stowed deep in my briefcase, I considered what it must have been like to have been raised under such a tyrant. My heart warmed somewhat toward young Sedgewick.

Back at St. Benedict's, furthermore, I saw that my words had evidently had some effect on the boy, for in the weeks that followed he continued on his struggling, uphill course. He passed two more quizzes, receiving an A minus on one of them. For his midterm project he produced an adequate papier-mâché rendering of Hadrian's gate, and in class he was less disruptive to the group of do-nothings among whom he sat, if indeed he was not in fact attentive.

Such, of course, are the honeyed morsels of a teacher's existence, those students who come, under one's own direction, from darkness into the light, and I admit that I might have taken a special interest that term in Sedgewick Bell. If I gave him the benefit of the doubt on his quizzes when he straddled two grades, if I began to call on him in class only for those questions I had reason to believe he could answer, then I was merely trying to encourage the nascent curiosity of a boy who, to all appearances, was struggling gamely from beneath the formidable umbra of his father.

The fall term was by then drawing to a close, and the boys had begun the frenzy of preliminary quizzes for the annual "Mr. Julius Caesar" competition. Here again, I suppose I was in my own way rooting for Sedgewick. "Mr. Julius Caesar" is a St. Benedict's tradition, held in reverence among the boys, the kind of mythic ritual that is the currency of a school like ours. It is a contest, held in two phases. The first is a narrowing maneuver, by means of a dozen written quizzes, from which three boys from the first form emerge victorious. The second is a public tournament, in which these three take the stage before the assembled student body and answer questions about ancient Rome until one alone emerges triumphant, as had Caesar himself from among Crassus and Pompey. Parents and graduates fill out the audience. In front of Mr. Woodbridge's office a plaque attests to the "Mr. Julius Caesars" of the previous half-century—a list that begins with John F. Dulles in 1901—and although the ritual might seem quaint to those who have not attended St. Benedict's, I can only say that in a school like ours one cannot overstate the importance of a public joust.

That year I had three obvious contenders: Fred Masoudi, who, as I intimated, was a somewhat gifted boy; Martin Blythe, a studious type; and Deepak Mehta, the son of a Bombay mathematician, who was dreadfully quiet but clearly my best student. It was Deepak, in fact, who on his own and entirely separate from the class had studied the disparate peoples, from the Carthaginians to the Egyptians, whom the Romans had conquered.

By the end of the narrowing quizzes, however, a surprising configuration had emerged: Sedgewick Bell had pulled himself to within a few points of third place in my class. This was when I made my first mistake. Although I should certainly have known better, I was impressed enough by his efforts that I broke one of the cardinal rules of teaching: I gave him an A on a quiz on which he had earned only a B, and in so doing, I leapfrogged him over Martin Blythe. On the fifteenth of March, when the three finalists took their seats on stage in front of the assembled population of the school, Sedgewick Bell was among them, and his father was among the audience.

The three boys had donned their togas for the event and were arranged around the dais, on which a pewter platter held the green silk garland that, at the end of the morning, I would place upon the brow of the winner. As the interrogator, I stood front row, center, next to Mr. Woodbridge.

"Which language was spoken by the Sabines?"

"Oscan," answered Fred Masoudi without hesitation.

"Who composed the Second Triumvirate?"

"Mark Antony, Octavian, and Marcus Aemilius Lepidus, sir," answered Deepak Mehta.

"Who was routed at Philippi?"

Sedgewick Bell's eyes showed no recognition. He lowered his head in his hands as though pushing himself to the limit of his intellect, and in the front row my heart dropped. Several boys in the audience began to twitter. Sedgewick's leg began to shake inside his toga. When he looked up again, I felt that it was I who had put him in this untenable position, I who had brought a tender bud too soon into the heat, and I wondered if he would ever forgive me; but then, without warning, he smiled slightly, folded his hands, and said, "Brutus and Cassius."

"Good," I said, instinctively. Then I gathered my poise. "Who deposed Romulus Augustulus, the last emperor of the Western Empire?"

"Odoacer," Fred Masoudi answered, then added, "in 476 A.D."

"Who introduced the professional army to Rome?"

"Gaius Marius, sir," answered Deepak Mehta, then himself added, "in 104 B.C."

When I asked Sedgewick his next question—Who was the leading Carthaginian general of the Second Punic War?—I felt some unease because the boys in the audience seemed to sense that I was favoring him with an easier examination. Nonetheless, his head sank into his hands, and he appeared once again to be straining the limits of his memory before he looked up and produced the obvious answer, "Hannibal."

I was delighted. Not only was he proving my gamble worthwhile but he was showing the twittering boys in the audience that, under fire, discipline produces accurate thought. By now they had quieted, and I had the sudden, heartening premonition that Sedgewick Bell was going to surprise us after all, that his tortoiselike deliberation would win him, by morning's end, the garland of laurel.

The next several rounds of questions proceeded much in the same manner as had the previous two. Deepak Mehta and Fred Masoudi answered without hesitation, and Sedgewick Bell did so only after a tedious and deliberate period of thought. What I realized, in fact, was that his style made for excellent theater. The parents, I could see, were impressed, and Mr. Woodbridge next to me, no doubt thinking about the next Annual Fund drive, was smiling broadly.

After a second-form boy had brought a glass of water to each of the contestants, I moved on to the next level of questions. These had been chosen for their difficulty, and on the first round Fred Masoudi fell out, not knowing the names of Augustus's children. He left the stage and moved back among his dim-witted pals in the audience. By the rule of clockwise progression the same question then went to Deepak Mehta, who answered it correctly, followed by the next one, which concerned King Jugurtha of Numidia. Then, because I had no choice, I had to ask Sedgewick Bell something difficult: "Which general had the support of the aristocrats in the civil war of 88 B.C.?"

To the side, I could see several parents pursing their lips and furrowing their brows, but Sedgewick Bell appeared to not even notice the greater difficulty of the query. Again he dropped his head into his hands. By now the audience expected his period of deliberation, and they sat quietly. One could hear the hum of the ventilation system and the dripping of the icicles outside. Sedgewick Bell cast his eyes downward, and it was at this moment that I realized he was cheating.

I had come to this job straight from my degree at Carleton College at the age of twenty-one, having missed enlistment due to myopia, and carrying with me the hope that I could give to my boys the more important vision that my classical studies had given to me. I knew that they responded best to challenge. I knew that a teacher who coddled them at that age would only hold them back, would keep them in the bosoms of their mothers so long that they would remain weak-minded through preparatory school and inevitably then through college. The best of my own teachers had been tyrants. I well remembered this. Yet at that moment I felt an inexplicable pity for the boy. Was it simply the humiliation we had both suffered at the hands of his father? I peered through my glasses at the stage and knew at once that he had attached the "Outline of Ancient Roman History" to the inside of his toga.

I don't know how long I stood there, between the school assembled behind me and the two boys seated in front, but after a period of internal deliberation, during which time I could hear the rising murmurs of the audience, I decided that in the long run it was best for Sedgewick Bell to be caught. Oh, how the battle is lost for want of a horse! I leaned to Mr. Woodbridge next to me and whispered, "I believe Sedgewick Bell is cheating."

"Ignore it," he whispered back.

"What?"

Of course, I have great respect for what Mr. Woodbridge did

for St. Benedict's in the years he was among us. A headmaster's world is a far more complex one than a teacher's, and it is historically inopportune to blame a life gone afoul on a single incident in childhood. However, I myself would have stood up for our principles had Mr. Woodbridge not at that point said, "Ignore it, Hundert, or look for another job."

Naturally, my headmaster's words startled me for a moment; but being familiar with the necessities of a boys' school, and having recently entertained my first thoughts about one day becoming a headmaster myself, I simply nodded when Sedge-wick Bell produced the correct answer, Lucius Cornelius Sulla. Then I went on to the next question, which concerned Scipio Africanus Major. Deepak Mehta answered it correctly, and I turned once again to Sedgewick Bell.

In a position of moral leadership, of course, compromise begets only more compromise, and although I know this now from my own experience, at the time I did so only from my study of history. Perhaps that is why I again found an untenable compassion muddying my thoughts. What kind of desperation would lead a boy to cheat on a public stage? His father and mother were well back in the crowded theater, but when I glanced behind me, my eye went instantly to them, as though they were indeed my own parents, out from Kansas City. "Who were the first emperors to reign over the divided Empire?" I asked Sedgewick Bell.

When one knows the magician's trick, the only wonder is in its obviousness, and as Sedgewick Bell lowered his head this time, I clearly saw the nervous flutter of his gaze directed into the toga. Indeed I imagined him scanning the entire "Outline," from Augustus to Jovian, pasted inside the twill, before coming to the answer, which pretending to ponder, he then spoke aloud: "Valentinian the First, and Valens."

Suddenly Senator Bell called out, "That's my boy!"

The crowd thundered, and I had the sudden, indefensible urge to steer the contest in young Sedgewick Bell's direction. In a few moments, however, from within the subsiding din, I heard the thin, accented voice of a woman speaking Deepak Mehta's name; and it was the presence of his mother, I suppose, that finally brought me to my senses. Deepak answered the next question, about Diocletian, correctly, and then I turned to Sedgewick Bell and asked him, "Who was Hamilcar Barca?"

Of course, it was only Deepak who knew that this answer was not in the "Outline," because Hamilcar Barca was a Phoenician general eventually routed by the Romans; it was only Deepak, as I have noted, who had bothered to study the conquered peoples. He briefly widened his eyes at me—in recognition? in gratitude? in disapproval?—while beside him Sedgewick Bell again lowered his head into his hands. After a long pause, Sedgewick asked me to repeat the question.

I did so, and after another long pause, he scratched his head. Finally, he said, "Jeez."

The boys in the audience laughed, but I turned and silenced them. Then I put the same question to Deepak Mehta, who answered it correctly, of course, and then received a round of applause that was polite but not sustained.

It was only as I mounted the stage to present Deepak with the garland of Laurel, however, that I glanced at Mr. Woodbridge and realized that he too had wanted me to steer the contest toward Sedgewick Bell. At the same moment, I saw Senator Bell making his way toward the rear door of the hall. Young Sedgewick stood limply to the side of me, and I believe I had my first inkling then of the mighty forces that would twist the life of that boy. I could only imagine his thoughts as he stood there on stage while his mother, struggling to catch up with the senator, vanished through the fire door at the back. By the next morning, our calligraphers would add Deepak Mehta's name to the plaque outside Mr. Woodbridge's office, and young Sedgewick Bell would begin his lifelong pursuit of missed glory.

Yet perhaps because of the disappointment I could see in Mr. Woodbridge's eyes, it somehow seemed that I was the one who had failed the boy, and as soon as the auditorium was empty, I left for his room. There I found him seated on the bed, still in his toga, gazing out the small window to the lacrosse fields. I could see the sheets of my "Outline" pressed against the inside of his garment.

"Well, young man," I said, knocking on the door frame, "that certainly was an interesting performance."

He turned around from the window and looked at me coldly. What he did next I have thought about many times over the years, the labyrinthine wiliness of it, and I can only attribute the precociousness of his maneuvering to the bitter education he must have received at home. As I stood before him in the doorway, Sedgewick Bell reached inside his cloak and one at a time lifted out the pages of my "Outline."

I stepped inside and closed the door. Every teacher knows a score of boys who do their best to be expelled; this is a cliché in a school like ours, but as soon as I closed the door to his room and he acknowledged the act with a feline smile, I knew that this was not Sedgewick Bell's intention at all.

"I knew you saw," he said.

"Yes, you are correct."

"How come you didn't say anything, eh, Mr. Hundert?"

"It's a complicated matter, Sedgewick."

"It's because my pop was there."

"It had nothing to do with your father."

"Sure, Mr. Hundert."

Frankly, I was at my wits' end, first from what Mr. Wood-bridge had said to me in the theater and now from the audacity of the boy's accusation. I myself went to the window then and let my eyes wander over the campus so that they would not have to engage the dark, accusatory gaze of Sedgewick Bell. What transpires in an act of omission like the one I had committed? I do not blame Mr. Woodbridge, of course, any more than a soldier can blame his captain. What had happened was that instead of enforcing my own code of morals, I had allowed Sedgewick Bell to sweep me summarily into his. I did not know at the time what an act of corruption I had committed, al-though what is especially chilling to me is that I believe that Sedgewick Bell, even at the age of thirteen, did.

He knew also, of course, that I would not pursue the matter, although I spent the ensuing several days contemplating a disciplinary action. Each time I summoned my resolve to sub-mit the boy's name to the honor committee, however, my conviction waned, for at these times I seemed to myself to be nothing more than one criminal turning in another. I fought this battle constantly—in my simple rooms, at the long, chipped table I governed in the dining hall, and at the dusty chalkboard before my classes. I felt like an exhausted swimmer trying to climb a slippery wall out of the sea.

Furthermore, I was alone in my predicament, for among a boarding school faculty, which is as perilous as a medieval court, one does not publicly discuss a boy's misdeeds. This is true even if the boy is not the son of a senator. In fact, the only teacher I decided to trust with my situation was Charles Ellerby, our new Latin instructor and a kindred lover of antiquity. I had liked Charles Ellerby as soon as we had met because he was a moralist of no uncertain terms, and indeed when I confided in him about Sedgewick Bell's behavior and Mr. Woodbridge's response, he suggested that it was my duty to circumvent our headmaster and speak directly to the boy's father. Of course, this made sense to me, even if I knew it would be difficult to do. I decided to speak to Senator Bell again.

Less than a week after I had begun to marshal my resolve, however, the senator himself called *me*. He proffered a few moments of small talk, asked after the gun he had given me, and then said gruffly, "Young man, my son tells me the Hannibal Barca question was not on the list he had to know."

Now, indeed, I was shocked. Even from young Sedgewick Bell I had not expected this audacity. "How deeply the viper is a viper," I said, before I could help myself.

"Excuse me?"

"The Phoenician general was *Hamilcar* Barca, sir, not Hannibal."

The senator paused. "My son tells me you asked him a question that was not on the list, which the Oriental fellow knew the answer to in advance. He feels you've been unfair, is all."

"It's a complex situation, sir," I said. I marshaled my will again by imagining what Charles Ellerby would do in the situation. However, no sooner had I resolved to confront the senator than it became perfectly clear to me that I lacked the character to do so. I believe this had long been clear to Sedgewick Bell.

"I'm sure it is complex," Senator Bell said, "But I assure you, there are situations more complex. Now, I'm not asking you to correct anything this time, you understand. My son has told me a great deal about you, Mr. Hundert. If I were you, I'd remember that."

"Yes, sir," I said, although by then I realized he had hung up.

And thus young Sedgewick Bell and I began an uneasy

compact that lasted out his days at St. Benedict's. He was a dismal student from that day forward, scratching at the very bottom of a class that was itself a far cry from the glorious yesteryear classes of John Dulles and Henry Stimson. His quizzes were abominations, and his essays were pathetic digestions of those of the boys sitting next to him. He chatted amiably in study hall, smoked cigarettes in the third-form linen room, and when called upon in class could be counted on to blink and stutter as if called upon from sleep.

But perhaps the glory days of St. Benedict's had already begun their wane, for even then, well before the large problems that beset us, no action was taken against the boy. For Charles Ellerby and me, he became a symbol, evidence of the first tendrils of moral rot that seemed to be twining among the posts and timbers of our school. Although we told nobody else of his secret, the boy's dim-witted recalcitrance soon succeeded in alienating all but the other students. His second- and third-form years passed as ingloriously as his first, and by the outset of his last with us he had grown to mythic infamy among the faculty members who had known the school in its days of glory.

He had grown physically larger as well, and now when I chanced upon him on the campus, he held his ground against my disapproving stare with a dark one of his own. To complicate matters, he had cultivated, despite his boorish character, an impressive popularity among his schoolmates, and it was only through the subtle intervention of several of his teachers that he had failed on two occasions to win the presidency of the student body. His stride had become a strut. His favor among the other boys, of course, had its origin in the strength of his physical features, in the precocious evil of his manner, and in the bellowing timbre of his voice, but unfortunately such crudities are all the more impressive to a group of boys living out of sight of their parents.

That is not to say that the faculty of St. Benedict's had given up hope for Sedgewick Bell. Indeed, a teacher's career is punctuated with difficult students like him, and despite the odds one could not help but root for his eventual rehabilitation. As did all the other teachers, I held out hope for Sedgewick Bell. In his fits of depravity and intellectual feebleness I continued to look for glimpses of discipline and progress.

By his fourth-form year, however, when I had become dean of seniors, it was clear that Sedgewick Bell would not change, at least not while he was at St. Benedict's. Despite his powerful station, he had not even managed to gain admission to the state university. It was with a sense of failure, then, finally, that I handed him his diploma in the spring of 1949, on an erected stage at the north end of the great field, on which he came forward, met my disapproving gaze with his own flat one, and trundled off to sit among his friends.

▲

It came as a surprise, then, when I learned in the Richmond *Gazette,* thirty-seven years later, of Sedgewick Bell's ascension to the chairmanship of EastAmerica Steel, at that time the second-largest corporation in America. I chanced upon the news one morning in the winter of 1987, the year of my great problems with St. Benedict's, while reading the newspaper in the east-lighted breakfast room of the assistant headmaster's house. St. Benedict's, as everyone knows, had fallen upon difficult times by then, and an unseemly aspect of my job was that I had to maintain a lookout for possible donors to the school. Forthwith, I sent a letter to Sedgewick Bell.

Apart from the five or six years in which a classmate had written to *The Benedictine* of his whereabouts, I had heard almost nothing about the boy since the year of his graduation. This was unusual, of course, as St. Benedict's makes a point of keeping abreast of its graduates, and I can only assume that his absence in the yearly alumni notes was due to an act of will on his own part. One wonders how much of the boy remained in the man. It is indeed a rare vantage that a St. Benedict's teacher holds, to have known our statesmen, our policymakers, and our captains of industry in their days of short pants and classroom pranks, and I admit that it was with some nostalgia that I composed the letter.

Since his graduation, of course, my career had proceeded with the steady ascension that the great schools have always afforded their dedicated teachers. Ten years after Sedgewick Bell's departure I had moved from dean of seniors to dean of the upper school, and after a decade there to dean of academics, a post that some would consider a demotion but that I seized with reverence because it afforded me the chance to make inroads on the minds of a generation. At the time, of course, the country was in the throes of a violent, peristaltic rejection of tradition, and I felt a particular urgency to my mission of staying a course that had led a century of boys through the rise and fall of ancient civilizations.

In those days our meetings of the faculty and trustees were rancorous affairs in which great pressure was exerted in attempts to alter the time-tested curriculum of the school. Planning a course was like going into battle, and hiring a new teacher was like crowning a king. Whenever one of our ranks retired or left for another school, the different factions fought tooth and nail to influence the appointment. I was the dean of academics, as I have noted, and these skirmishes naturally were waged around my foxhole. For the lesser appointments I often feinted to gather leverage for the greater ones, whose campaigns I fought with abandon.

At one point especially, midway through that decade in

which our country had lost its way, St. Benedict's arrived at a crossroads. The chair of humanities had retired, and a pitched battle over his replacement developed between Charles Ellerby and a candidate from outside. A meeting ensued in which my friend and this other man spoke to the assembled faculty and trustees, and though I will not go into detail, I will say that the outside candidate felt that, because of the advances in our society, history had become little more than a relic.

Oh, what dim-sighted times those were! The two camps sat on opposite sides of the chapel as speakers took the podium one after another to wage war. The controversy quickly became a forum concerning the relevance of the past. Teacher after teacher debated the import of what we in history had taught for generations, and assertion after assertion was met with boos and applause. Tempers blazed. One powerful member of the board had come to the meeting in blue jeans and a tie-dyed shirt, and after we had been arguing for several hours and all of us were exhausted, he took the podium and challenged me personally, right then and there, to debate with him the merits of Roman history.

He was not an ineloquent man, and he chose to speak his plea first, so that by the time he had finished his attack against antiquity, I sensed that my battle on behalf of Charles Ellerby, and of history itself, was near to lost. My heart was gravely burdened, for if we could not win our point here among teachers, then among whom indeed could we win it? The room was silent, and on the other side of the chapel our opponents were gathering nearer to one another in the pews.

When I rose to defend my calling, however, I also sensed that victory was not beyond my reach. I am not a particularly eloquent orator, but as I took my place at the chancel rail in the amber glow of the small rose window above us, I was braced by the sudden conviction that the great men of history had sent me forward to preserve their deeds. Charles Ellerby looked up at me biting his lip, and suddenly I remembered the answer I had written long ago in *The Crier*. Its words flowed as though unbidden from my tongue, and when I had finished, I knew that we had won. It was my proudest moment at St. Benedict's.

Although the resultant split among the faculty was an egregious one, Charles Ellerby secured the appointment, and together we were able to do what I had always dreamed of doing: We redoubled our commitment to classical education. In times of upheaval, of course, adherence to tradition is all the more important, and perhaps this was why St. Benedict's was brought intact through that decade and the one that followed. Our fortunes lifted and dipped with the gentle rhythm to which I had long ago grown accustomed. Our boys won sporting events and prizes, endured minor scandals and occasional tragedies, and then passed on to good colleges. Our endowment rose when the government was in the hands of Republicans, as did the caliber of our boys when it was in the hands of Democrats. Senator Bell declined from prominence, and within a few years I read that he had passed away. In time, I was made assistant headmaster. Indeed it was not until a few years ago that anything out of the ordinary happened at all, for it was then, in the late 1980s, that some ill-advised investments were made and our endowment suffered a decline.

Mr. Woodbridge had by this time reached the age of seventy-four, and although he was a vigorous man, one Sunday morning in May while the school waited for him in chapel he died open-eyed in his bed. Immediately there occurred a Byzantine struggle for succession. There is nothing wrong with admitting that by then I myself coveted the job of headmaster, for one does not remain five decades at a school without becoming deeply attached to its fate; but Mr. Woodbridge's death had come suddenly, and I had not yet begun the preparations for my bid. I was, of course, no longer a young man. I suppose, in fact, that I lost my advantage here by underestimating my opponents, who indeed were younger, as Caesar had done with Brutus and Cassius.

I should not have been surprised, then, when after several days of maneuvering, my principal rival turned out to be Charles Ellerby. For several years, I discovered, he had been conducting his own internecine campaign for the position, and although I had always counted him as my ally and my friend, in the first meeting of the board he rose and spoke accusations against me. He said that I was too old, that I had failed to change with the times, that my method of pedagogy might have been relevant forty years ago but that it was not today. He stood and said that a headmaster needed vigor and that I did not have it. Although I watched him the entire time he spoke, he did not once look back at me.

I was wounded, of course, both professionally and in the hidden part of my heart in which I had always counted Charles Ellerby as a companion in my lifelong search for the magnificence of the past. When several of the older teachers booed him, I felt cheered. At this point I saw that I was not alone in my bid, merely behind, and so I left the meeting without coming to my own defense. Evening had come, and I walked to the dining commons in the company of allies.

How it is, when fighting for one's life, to eat among children! As the boys in their school blazers passed around the platters of fish sticks and the bowls of sliced bread, my heart was pierced with their guileless grace. How soon, I wondered, would they see the truth of the world? How long before they would understand that it was not dates and names that I had always meant to teach them? Not one of them seemed to notice what had descended like thunderheads above their faculty. Not one of them seemed unable to eat.

After dinner I returned to the assistant headmaster's house in order to plot my course and confer with those I still considered allies, but before I could begin my preparations, there was a knock at the door. Charles Ellerby stood there, red in the cheeks. "May I ask you some questions?" he said breathlessly.

"It is I who ought to ask them of you" was my answer.

He came in without being asked and took a seat at my table. "You've never been married, am I correct, Hundert?"

"Look, Ellerby, I've been at St. Benedict's since you were in prep school yourself."

"Yes, yes," he said, in an exaggeration of boredom. Of course, he knew as well as I that I had never married nor started a family because history itself had always been enough for me. He rubbed his head and appeared to be thinking. To this day I wonder how he knew about what he said next, unless Sedgewick Bell had somehow told him the story of my visit to the senator. "Look," he said. "There's a rumor you keep a pistol in your desk drawer."

"Hogwash."

"Will you open it for me," he said, pointing there.

"No, I will not. I have been a dean here for twenty years."

"Are you telling me there is no pistol in this house?"

He then attempted to stare me down. We had known each other for the good part of both of our lives, however, and the bid withered. At that point, in fact, as his eyes fell in submission to my determined gaze, I believe the headmastership became mine. It is a largely unexplored element of history, of course, and one that has long fascinated me, that a great deal of political power and thus a great deal of the arc of nations arises not from intellectual advancements nor social imperatives but from the simple battle of wills among men at tables, such as had just occurred between Charles Ellerby and me.

Instead of opening the desk and brandishing the weapon, however, which of course meant nothing to me but no doubt would have seized the initiative from Ellerby, I denied to him its existence. Why, I do not know; for I was a teacher of history, and was not the firearm its greatest engine? Ellerby, on the other hand, was simply a gadfly to the passing morals of the time. He gathered his things and left my house.

That evening I took the pistol from my drawer. A margin of rust had appeared along the filigreed handle, and despite the ornate workmanship I saw clearly now that in its essence the weapon was ill-proportioned and blunt, the crude instrument of a violent, historically meager man. I had not even wanted it when the irascible demagogue Bell had foisted it upon me, and I had only taken it out of some vague sentiment that a pistol might eventually prove decisive. I suppose I had always imagined firing it someday in a moment of drama. Yet now here it stood before me in a moment of torpor. I turned it over and cursed it.

That night I took it from the drawer again, hid it in the pocket of my overcoat, and walked to the far end of the campus, where I crossed the marsh a good mile from my house, removed my shoes, and stepped into the babbling shallows of the Passamic. *The die is cast*, I said, and I threw it twenty yards out into the water. The last impediment to my headmastership had been hurdled, and by the time I came ashore, walked back whistling to my front door, and changed for bed, I was ecstatic.

Yet that night I slept poorly, and in the morning when I rose and went to our faculty meeting, I felt that the mantle of my fortitude had slipped somehow from my shoulders. How hushed is demise! In the hall outside the faculty room, most of the teachers filed by without speaking to me, and once inside, I became obsessed with the idea that I had missed this most basic lesson of the past, that conviction is the alpha and the omega of authority. Now I see that I was doomed the moment I threw that pistol in the water, for that is when I lost my conviction. It was as though Sedgewick Bell had risen, all these years later, to drag me down again. Indeed, once the meeting had begun, the older faculty members shrunk back from their previous support of my bid, and the younger ones encircled me as though I were a limping animal. There might as well have been a dagger among the cloaks. By four o'clock that afternoon Charles Ellerby, a fellow antiquarian whose job I had once helped secure, had been named headmaster, and by the end of that month he had asked me to retire.

And so I was preparing to end my days at St. Benedict's when I received Sedgewick Bell's response to my letter. It was well written, which I noted with pleasure, and contained no trace of rancor, which is what every teacher hopes to see in the maturation of his disagreeable students. In closing he asked me to call him at EastAmerica Steel, and I did so that afternoon. When I gave my name first to one secretary and then to a second, and after that, moments later, heard Sedgewick's artfully guileless greeting, I instantly recalled speaking to his father some forty years before.

After small talk, including my condolences about his father, he told me that the reason he had replied to my letter was that he had often dreamed of holding a rematch of "Mr. Julius Caesar," and that he was now willing to donate a large sum of money to St. Benedict's if I would agree to administer the event. Naturally, I assumed he was joking and passed off the idea with a comment about how funny it was, but Sedgewick Bell repeated the invitation. He wanted very much to be on-stage again with Deepak Mehta and Fred Masoudi. I suppose I should not have been surprised, for it is precisely this sort of childhood slight that will drive a great figure. I told him that I was about to retire. He expressed sympathy but then suggested that the arrangement could be ideal, as now I would no doubt have time to prepare. Then he said that at this station in his life he could afford whatever he wanted materially—with all that this implied, of course, concerning his donation to the Annual Fund—but that more than anything else, he desired the chance to reclaim his intellectual honor. I suppose I was flattered.

Of course, he also offered a good sum of money to me personally. Although I had until then led a life in which finances were never more than a distant concern, I was keenly aware that my time in the school's houses and dining halls was coming to an end. On the one hand, it was not my burning aspiration to secure an endowment for the reign of Charles Ellerby; on the other hand, I needed the money, and I felt a deep loyalty to the school regarding the Annual Fund. That evening I began to prepare my test.

As assistant headmaster I had not taught my beloved Roman history in many years, so that poring through my reams of notes was like returning at last to my childhood home. I stopped here and there among the files. I reread the term paper of young Derek Bok entitled "The Search of Diogenes" and the scrawled one of James Watson called "Archimedes' Method." Among the art projects I found John Updike's reproduction of the Obelisk of Cleopatra and a charcoal drawing of the Baths of Caracala by the abstract expressionist Robert Motherwell, unfortunately torn in two and no longer worth anything.

I had always been a diligent note taker, furthermore, and I believe that what I came up with was a surprisingly accurate reproduction of the subjects on which I had once quizzed Fred Masoudi, Deepak Mehta, and Sedgewick Bell, nearly half a century before. It took me only two evenings to gather enough material for the task, although in order not to appear eager, I waited several days before sending off another letter to Sedgewick Bell. He called me soon after.

It is indeed a surprise to one who toils for his own keep to see the formidable strokes with which our captains of industry demolish the tasks before them. The morning after talking to Sedgewick Bell I received calls from two of his secretaries, a social assistant, and a woman at a New York travel agency, who confirmed the arrangements for late July, two months hence. The event was to take place on an island off the Outer Banks of Carolina that belonged to EastAmerica Steel, and I sent along a list from the St. Benedict's archives so that everyone in Sedgewick Bell's class would be invited.

I was not prepared, however, for the days of retirement that intervened. What little remained of that school year passed speedily in my preoccupation, and before I knew it, the boys were taking their final exams. I tried not to think about my future. At the commencement exercises in June a small section of the ceremony was spent in my honor, but it was presided over by Charles Ellerby and gave rise to a taste of copper in my throat. "And thus we bid adieu," he began, "to our beloved Mr. Hundert." He gazed out over the lectern, extended his arm in my direction, and proceeded to give a nostalgic rendering of my years at the school to the audience of jacketed businessmen, parasoled ladies, students in St. Benedict's blazers, and children in church suits, who, like me, were squirming at the meretriciousness of the man.

Yet how quickly it was over! Awards were presented, "Hail, Fair Benedict's" was sung, and as the birches began to lean their narrow shadows against the distant edge of the marsh the seniors came forward to receive their diplomas. The mothers wept, the alumni stood misty-eyed, and the graduates threw their hats into the air. Afterward everyone dispersed for the headmaster's reception.

I wish now that I had made an appearance there, for to have missed it, the very last one of my career, was a far more grievous blow to me than to Charles Ellerby. Furthermore, the handful of senior boys who over their tenure had been pierced by the bee sting of history no doubt missed my presence or at least wondered at its lack. I spent the remainder of the afternoon in my house, and the evening walking out along the marsh, where the smell of woodsmoke from a farmer's bonfire and the distant sounds of the gathered celebrants filled me with the great, sad pride of teaching. My boys were passing once again into the world without me.

The next day, of course, parents began arriving to claim their children; jitney buses ferried students to airports and train stations; the groundsman went around pulling up lacrosse goals and baseball bleachers, hauling the long black sprinkler hoses behind his tractor into the fields. I spent most of that day and the next one sitting at the desk in my study, watching through the window as the school wound down like a clock spring toward the strange, bird-filled calm of that second afternoon of my retirement, when all the boys had left and I was alone, once again, in the eerie quiet of summer. I own few things besides my files and books; I packed them, and the next day the groundsman drove me into Woodmere.

There I found lodging in a splendid Victorian rooming house run by a descendant of Nat Turner who joked, when I told her that I was a newly retired teacher, about how the house had always welcomed escaped slaves. I was surprised at how heartily I laughed at this, which had the benefit of putting me instantly on good terms with the landlady. We negotiated a monthly rent, and I went upstairs to set about charting a new life for myself. I was sixty-eight years old—yes, perhaps, too old to be headmaster—but I could still walk three miles before dinner and did so the first afternoon of my freedom. However, by evening my spirits had taken a beating.

Fortunately, there was the event to prepare for, as I fear that without it, those first days and nights would have been unbearable. I pored again and again over my old notes, extracting devilish questions from the material. But this only occupied a few hours of the day, and by late morning my eyes would grow weary. Objectively speaking, the start of that summer should have been no different from the start of any other; yet it was. Passing my reflection in the hallway mirror on my way down to dinner, I would think to myself, *Is that you?*, and on the way back up to my room, *What now?* I wrote letters to my brothers and sister and to several of my former boys. The days crawled by. I reintroduced myself to the town librarian. I made the acquaintance of a retired railroad man who liked as much as I did to sit on the grand, screened porch of that house. I took the bus into Washington a few times to spend the day in museums.

But as the summer progressed, a certain dread began to form in my mind, which I tried through the diligence of walking, museum-going, and reading, to ignore; that is, I began to fear that Sedgewick Bell had forgotten about the event. The thought would occur to me in the midst of the long path along the outskirts of town; and as I reached the Passamic, took my break, and then started back again toward home, I would battle with my urge to contact the man. Several times I went to the telephone downstairs in the rooming house, and twice I wrote out letters that I did not send. Why would he go through all the trouble just to mock me, I thought; but then I would recall the circumstances of his tenure at St. Benedict's, and a darker gloom would descend upon me. I began to have second thoughts about events that had occurred half a century before: Should I have confronted him in the midst of the original contest? Should I never even have leapfrogged another boy to get him there? Should I have spoken up to the senator?

In early July, however, Sedgewick Bell's secretary finally did call, and I felt that I had been given a reprieve. She apologized for her tardiness, asked me more questions about my taste in food and lodging, and then informed me of the date, three weeks later, when a car would call to take me to the airport in Williamsburg. An EastAmerica jet would fly me from there to Charlotte, from whence I was to be picked up by helicopter.

Helicopter! Less than a month later I stood before the craft, which was painted head to tail in EastAmerica's green and gold insignia, polished to a shine, with a six-man passenger bay and red-white-and-blue sponsons over the wheels. One does not remain at St. Benedict's for five decades without gaining a certain familiarity with privilege, yet as it lifted me off the pad in Charlotte, hovered for a moment, then lowered its nose and turned eastward over the gentle hills and then the chopping slate of the sea channel, I felt a headiness that I had never known before; it was what Augustus Caesar must have felt millennia ago, carried head-high on a litter past the Tiber. I clutched my notes to my chest. Indeed, I wondered what my life might have been like if I had felt this just once in my youth. The rotors buzzed like a swarm of bees above us. On the island I was shown to a suite of rooms in a high corner of the lodge, with windows and balconies overlooking the sea.

For a conference on the future of childhood education or the plight of America's elderly, of course, you could not get one-tenth of these men to attend, but for a privileged romp on a private island it had merely been a matter of making the arrangements. I stood at the window of my room and watched the helicopter ferry back and forth across the channel, disgorging on the island a Who's Who of America's largest corporations, universities, and organs of policy.

Oh, but what it was to see the boys! After a time I made my way back out to the airstrip, and whenever the craft touched down on the landing platform and one or another of my old students ducked out, clutching his suit lapel as he ran clear of the snapping rotors, I was struck anew with how great a privilege my profession had been.

That evening all of us ate together in the lodge, and the boys toasted me and took turns coming to my table, where several times one or another of them had to remind me to continue eating my food. Sedgewick Bell ambled over and with a charming air of modesty showed me the flash cards of Roman history that he'd been keeping in his desk at EastAmerica. Then, shedding his modesty, he went to the podium and produced a long and raucous toast, referring to any number of pranks and misdeeds at St. Benedict's that I had never even heard of but that the chorus of boys greeted with stamps and whistles. At a quarter to nine they all dropped their forks onto the floor, and I fear that tears came to my eyes.

The most poignant part of all, however, was how plainly the faces of the men still showed the eager expressiveness of the first-form boys of forty-one years ago. Martin Blythe had lost half his leg as an officer in Korea, and now, among his classmates, he tried to hide his lurching stride, but he wore the same knitted brow that he used to wear in my classroom; Deepak Mehta, who had become a professor of Asian history, walked with a slight stoop, yet he still turned his eyes downward when spoken to; Fred Masoudi seemed to have fared physically better than his mates, bouncing about in the Italian suit and alligator shoes of the advertising industry, yet he was still drawn immediately to the other do-nothings from his class.

But of course it was Sedgewick Bell who commanded everyone's attention. He had grown stout across the middle and bald over the crown of his head, and I saw in his ear, although it was artfully concealed, the flesh-colored bulb of a hearing aid; yet he walked among the men like a prophet. Their faces grew animated when he approached, and at the tables I could see them competing for his attention. He patted one on the back, whispered in the ear of another, gripped hands and grasped shoulders and kissed the wives on the lips. His walk was firm and imbued not with the seriousness of his post, it seemed to me, but with the ease of it, so that his stride among the tables was jocular. He was the host and clearly in his element. His laugh was voluble.

I went to sleep early that evening so that the boys could enjoy themselves downstairs in the saloon, and as I lay in bed, I listened to their songs and revelry. It had not escaped my attention, of course, that they no doubt spent some time mocking me, but this is what one grows to expect in my post, and indeed it was part of the reason I left them alone. Although I was tempted to walk down and listen from outside the theater, I did not.

The next day was spent walking the island's serpentine spread of coves and beaches, playing tennis on the grass court, and paddling in wooden boats on the small, inland lake behind the lodge. How quickly one grows accustomed to luxury! Men and women lounged on the decks and beaches and patios, sunning like seals, gorging themselves on the largesse of their host.

As for me, I barely had a moment to myself, for the boys

took turns at my entertainment. I walked with Deepak Mehta along the beach and succeeded in getting him to tell me the tale of his rise through academia to a post at Columbia University. Evidently his career had taken a toll, for although he looked healthy enough, he told me that he had recently had a small heart attack. It was not the type of thing one talked about with a student, however, so I let his revelation pass without comment. Later Fred Masoudi brought me onto the tennis court and tried to teach me to hit a ball, an activity that drew a crowd of boisterous guests to the stands. They roared at Fred's theatrical antics and cheered and stomped their feet whenever I sent one back across the net. In the afternoon Martin Blythe took me out in a rowboat.

St. Benedict's, of course, has always had a more profound effect than most schools on the lives of its students, yet nonetheless it was strange that once in the center of the pond, where he had rowed us with his lurching stroke, Martin Blythe set down the oars in their locks and told me he had something he'd always meant to ask me.

"Yes," I said.

He brushed back his hair with his hand. "*I* was supposed to be the one up there with Deepak and Fred, wasn't I, sir?"

"Don't tell me you're still thinking about that."

"It's just that I've sometimes wondered what happened."

"Yes, you should have been," I said.

Oh, how little we understand of men if we think that their childhood slights are forgotten! He smiled. He did not press the subject further, and while I myself debated the merits of explaining why I had passed him over for Sedgewick Bell forty-one years before, he pivoted the boat around and brought us back to shore. The confirmation of his suspicions was enough to satisfy him, it seemed, so I said nothing more. He had been an air force major in our country's endeavors on the Korean peninsula, yet as he pulled the boat onto the beach, I had the clear feeling of having saved him from some torment.

Indeed, that evening when the guests had gathered in the lodge's small theater, and Deepak Mehta, Fred Masoudi, and Sedgewick Bell had taken their seats for the reenactment of "Mr. Julius Caesar," I noticed an ease in Martin Blythe's face that I believe I had never seen in it before. His brow was not knit, and he had crossed his legs so that above one sock we could clearly see the painted wooden calf.

It was then that I noticed that the boys who had paid the most attention to me that day were in fact the ones sitting before me on the stage. How dreadful a thought this was—that they had indulged me to gain advantage—but I put it from my mind and stepped to the microphone. I had spent the late afternoon reviewing my notes, and the first rounds of questions were called from memory.

The crowd did not fail to notice the feat. There were whistles and stomps when I named fifteen of the first sixteen emperors in order and asked Fred Masoudi to produce the one I had left out. There was applause when I spoke Caesar's words, *Il Iacta alea esto,* and then, continuing in carefully pronounced Latin, asked Sedgewick Bell to recall the circumstances of their utterance. He had told me that afternoon of the months he had spent preparing, and as I was asking the question, he smiled. The boys had not worn togas, of course—although I personally feel they might have—yet the situation was familiar enough that I felt a rush of unease as Sedgewick Bell's smile then waned and he hesitated several moments before answering. But this time, forty-one years later, he looked straight out into the audience and spoke his answers with the air of a scholar.

It was not long before Fred Masoudi had dropped out, of

course, but then, as it had before, the contest proceeded neck and neck between Sedgewick Bell and Deepak Mehta. I asked Sedgewick Bell about Caesar's battles at Pharsalus and Thapsus, about the shift of power to Constantinople, and about the war between the patricians and the plebeians; I asked Deepak Mehta about the Punic wars, the conquest of Italy, and the fall of the Republic. Deepak of course had an advantage, for certainly he had studied this material at university, but I must say that the straightforward determination of Sedgewick Bell had begun to win my heart. I recalled the bashful manner in which he had shown me his flash cards at dinner the night before, and as I stood now before the microphone I seemed to be in the throes of an affection for him that had long been under wraps.

"What year were the Romans routed at Lake Trasimene?" I asked him.

He paused. "Two hundred seventeen B.C., I believe."

"Which general later became Scipio Africanus Major?"

"Publius Cornelius Scipio, sir," Deepak Mehta answered softly.

It does not happen as often as one might think that an unintelligent boy becomes an intelligent man, for in my own experience the love of thought is rooted in an age long before adolescence; yet Sedgewick Bell now seemed to have done just that. His answers were spoken with the composed demeanor of a scholar. There is no one I like more, of course, than the man who is moved by the mere fact of history, and as I contemplated the next question to him I wondered if I had indeed exaggerated the indolence of his boyhood. Was it true, perhaps, that he had simply not come into his element yet while at St. Benedict's? He peered intently at me from the stage, his elbows on his knees. I decided to ask him a difficult question. "Chairman Bell," I said, "which tribes invaded Rome in 102 B.C.?"

His eyes went blank and he curled his shoulders in his suit. Although he was by then one of the most powerful men in America, and although moments before that I had been rejoicing in his discipline, suddenly I saw him on that stage once again as a frightened boy. How powerful is memory! And once again, I feared that it was I who had betrayed him. He brought his hand to his head to think.

"Take your time, sir," I offered.

There were murmurs in the audience. He distractedly touched the side of his head. Man's character is his fate, says Heraclitus, and at that moment, as he brushed his hand down over his temple, I realized that the flesh-colored device in his ear was not a hearing aid but a transmitter through which he was receiving the answers to my questions. Nausea rose in me. Of course I had no proof, but was it not exactly what I should have expected? He touched his head once again and appeared to be deep in thought, and I knew it as certainly as if he had shown me. "The Teutons," he said, haltingly, "and—I'll take a stab here—the Cimbri?"

I looked for a long time at him. Did he know at that point what I was thinking? I cannot say, but after I had paused as long as I could bear to in front of that crowd, I cleared my throat and granted that he was right. Applause erupted. He shook it off with a wave of his hand. I knew that it was my duty to speak up. I knew it was my duty as a teacher to bring him clear of the moral dereliction in which I myself had been his partner, yet at the same time I felt myself adrift in the tide of my own vacillation and failure. The boy had somehow got hold of me again. He tried to quiet the applause with a wave of his hand, but this gesture only caused the clapping to increase, and I am afraid to say that it was merely the sound of a throng of boisterous men that finally prevented me from making my stand. Quite suddenly I was aware that this was not the situation I had known at St. Benedict's School. We were guests now of a significant man on his splendid estate, and to expose him would be a serious act indeed. I turned and quieted the crowd.

From the chair next to Sedgewick Bell, Deepak Mehta merely looked at me, his eyes dark and resigned. Perhaps he too had just realized, or perhaps in fact he had long known, but in any case I simply asked him the next question; after he answered it, I could do nothing but put another before Sedgewick Bell. Then Deepak again, then Sedgewick, and again to Deepak, and it was only then, on the third round after I had discovered the ploy, that an idea came to me. When I returned to Sedgewick Bell, I asked him, "Who was Shutruk-Nahhunte?"

A few boys in the crowd began to laugh, and when Sedgewick Bell took his time thinking about the answer, more in the audience joined in. Whoever was the mercenary professor talking in his ear, it was clear to me that he would not know the answer to this one, for if he had not gone to St. Benedict's School he would never have heard of Shutruk-Nahhunte; and in a few moments, sure enough, I saw Sedgewick Bell begin to grow uncomfortable. He lifted his pant leg and scratched at his sock. The laughter increased, and then I heard the wives, who had obviously never lived in a predatory pack, trying to stifle their husbands. "Come on, Bell!" someone shouted, "Look at the damn door!" Laughter erupted again.

How can it be that for a moment my heart bled for him? He, too, tried to laugh, but only halfheartedly. He shifted in his seat, shook his arms loose in his suit, looked uncomprehendingly out at the snickering crowd, then braced his chin and said, "Well, I guess if Deepak knows the answer to this one, then it's *his* ball game."

Deepak's response was nearly lost in the boisterous stamps

and whistles that followed, for I am sure that every boy but Sedgewick recalled Henry Stimson's tablet above the door of my classroom. Yet what was strange was that I felt disappointment. As Deepak Mehta smiled, spoke the answer, and stood from his chair, I watched confusion and then a flicker of panic cross the face of Sedgewick Bell. He stood haltingly. How clear it was to me then that the corruption in his character had always arisen from fear, and I could not help remembering that as his teacher I had once tried to convince him of his stupidity. I cursed that day. But then in a moment he summoned a smile, called me up to the stage, and crossed theatrically to congratulate the victor.

How can I describe the scene that took place next? I suppose I was naïve to think that this was the end of the evening—or even the point of it—for after Sedgewick Bell had brought forth a trophy for Deepak Mehta, and then one for me as well, an entirely different cast came across his features. He strode once again to the podium and asked for the attention of the guests. He tapped sharply on the microphone. Then he leaned his head forward, and in a voice that I recognized from long ago on the radio, a voice in whose deft leaps from boom to whisper I heard the willow-tree drawl of his father, he launched into an address about the problems of our country. He had the orator's gift of dropping his volume at the moment when a less gifted man would have raised it. *We have opened our doors to all the world,* he said, his voice thundering, then pausing, then plunging nearly to a murmur, *and now the world has stripped us bare.* He gestured with his hands. The men in the audience, first laughing, now turned serious. *We have given away too much for too long,* he said. *We have handed our fiscal leadership to men who don't care about the taxpayers of our country, and our moral course to those who no longer understand our role in history.*

Although he gestured to me here, I could not return his gaze. *We have abandoned the moral education of our families.* Scattered applause drifted up from his classmates, and here, of course, I almost spoke. *We have left our country adrift on dangerous seas.* Now the applause was more hearty. Then he quieted his voice again, dropped his head as though in supplication, and announced that he was running for the United States Senate.

Why was I surprised? I should not have been, for since childhood the boy had stood so near to the mantle of power that its shadow must have been as familiar to him as his boyhood home. Virtue had no place in the palaces he had known. I was ashamed when I realized he had contrived the entire rematch of "Mr. Julius Caesar" for no reason other than to gather his classmates for donations, yet still I chastened myself for not realizing his ambition before. In his oratory, in his physical presence, in his conviction, he had always possessed the gifts of a leader, and now he was using them. I should have expected this from the first day he stood in his short-pants suit in the doorway of my classroom and silenced my students. He already wielded a potent role in the affairs of our county; he enjoyed the presumption of his family name; he was blindly ignorant of history and therefore did not fear his role in it. Of course it was exactly the culmination I should long ago have seen. The crowd stood cheering.

As soon as the clapping abated, a curtain was lifted behind him and a band struck up "Dixie." Waiters appeared at the side doors, a dance platform was unfolded in the orchestra pit, and Sedgewick Bell jumped down from the stage into the crowd of his friends. They clamored around him. He patted shoulders, kissed wives, whispered and laughed and nodded his head. I saw checkbooks come out. The waiters carried champagne on trays at their shoulders, and at the edge of the dance floor the women set down their purses and stepped into the arms of their husbands. When I saw this I ducked out a side door and returned to the lodge, for the abandon with which the guests were dancing was an unbearable counterpart to the truth I knew. One can imagine my feelings. I heard the din late into the night.

Needless to say, I resolved to avoid Sedgewick Bell for the remainder of my stay. How my mind raced that night through humanity's endless history of injustice, depravity, and betrayal! I could not sleep, and several times I rose and went to the window to listen to the revelry. Standing at the glass, I felt like the spurned sovereign in the castle tower, looking down from his balcony onto the procession of the false potentate.

Yet, sure enough, my conviction soon began to wane. No sooner had I resolved to avoid my host than I began to doubt the veracity of my secret knowledge about him. Other thoughts came to me. How, in fact, had I been so sure of what he'd done? What proof had I at all? Amid the distant celebrations of the night, my conclusion began to seem farfetched, and by the quiet of the morning I was muddled. I did not go to breakfast. As boy after boy stopped by my rooms to wish me well, I assiduously avoided commenting on either Sedgewick Bell's performance or on his announcement for the Senate. On the beach that day I endeavored to walk by myself, for by then I trusted neither my judgment of the incident nor my discretion with the boys. I spent the afternoon alone in a cove across the island.

I did not speak to Sedgewick Bell that entire day. I managed to avoid him, in fact, until the next evening, by which time all but a few of the guests had left, when he came to bid farewell as I stood on the tarmac awaiting the helicopter for the mainland. He walked out and motioned for me to stand back from the platform, but I pretended not to hear him and kept my eyes up to the sky. Suddenly the shining craft swooped in from beyond the wavebreak, churning the channel into a boil, pulled up in a hover and then touched down on its flag-colored sponsons before us. The wind and noise could have thrown a man to the ground, and Sedgewick Bell seemed to pull at me like a magnet, but I did not retreat. It was he, finally, who ran out to me. He gripped his lapels, ducked his head, and offered me his hand. I took it tentatively, the rotors whipping our jacket sleeves. I had been expecting this moment and had decided the night before what I was going to say. I leaned toward him. "How long have you been hard of hearing?" I asked.

His smile dropped. I cannot imagine what I had become in the mind of that boy. "Very good, Hundert," he said. "Very good. I thought you might have known."

My vindication was sweet, although now I see that it meant little. By then I was on the ladder of the helicopter, but he pulled me toward him again and looked darkly into my eyes. "And I see that *you* have not changed either," he said.

Well, had I? As the craft lifted off and turned westward toward the bank of clouds that hid the distant shoreline, I analyzed the situation with some care. The wooden turrets of the lodge grew smaller and then were lost in the trees, and I found it easier to think then, for everything on that island had been imbued with the sheer power of the man. I relaxed a bit in my seat. One could say that in this case I indeed had acted properly, for is it not the glory of our legal system that acquitting a guilty man is less heinous than convicting an innocent one? At the time of the contest, I certainly had no proof of Sedgewick Bell's behavior.

Yet back in Woodmere, as I have intimated, I found myself with a great deal of time on my hands, and it was not long before the incident began to replay itself in my mind. Following the wooded trail toward the river or sitting in the breeze at dusk on the porch, I began to see that a different ending would have better served us all. Conviction had failed me again. I was well aware of the foolish consolation of my thoughts, yet I vividly imagined what I should have done. I heard myself speaking up; I saw my resolute steps to his chair on the stage, then the insidious, flesh-colored device in my palm, held up to the crowd; I heard him stammering.

As if to mock my inaction, however, stories of his electoral effort soon began to appear in the papers. It was a year of spite and rancor in our country's politics, and the race in West Virginia was less a campaign than a brawl between gladiators. The incumbent was as versed in treachery as Sedgewick Bell, and over my morning tea I followed their battles. Sedgewick Bell called him "a liar when he speaks and a crook when he acts," and he called Sedgewick Bell worse. A fistfight erupted when their campaigns crossed at an airport.

I was revolted by the spectacle, but of course I was also intrigued, and I cannot deny that although I was rooting for the incumbent, a part of me was also cheered at each bit of news chronicling Sedgewick Bell's assault on his lead. Oh, why was this so? Are we all, at base, creatures without virtue? Is fervor the only thing we follow?

Needless to say, that fall had been a difficult one in my life, especially those afternoons when the St. Benedict's bus roared by the guest house in Woodmere taking the boys to track meets, and perhaps the Senate race was nothing more than a healthy distraction for me. Indeed, I needed distractions. To witness the turning of the leaves and to smell the apples in their barrels without hearing the sound of a hundred boys in the fields, after all, was almost more than I could bear. My walks had grown longer, and several times I had crossed the river and ventured to the far end of the marsh, from where in the distance I could make out the blurred figures of St. Benedict's. I knew this was not good for me, and perhaps that is why, in late October of that year when I read that Sedgewick Bell would be making a campaign stop at a coal-miners' union hall near the Virginia border, I decided to go hear him speak.

Perhaps by then the boy had become an obsession for me—I will admit this, for I am as aware as anyone that time is but the thinnest bandage for our wounds—but on the other hand, the race had grown quite close and would have been of natural interest to anyone. Sedgewick Bell had drawn himself up from underdog to challenger. Now it was clear that the election hinged on the votes of labor, and Sedgewick Bell, though he was the son of aristocrats and the chairman of a formidable corporation, began to cast himself as a champion of the working man. From newspaper reports I gleaned that he was helped along by the power of his voice and bearing, and I could easily imagine these men turning to him. I well knew the charisma of the boy.

The day arrived, and I packed a lunch and made the trip. As the bus wound west along the river valley, I envisioned the scene ahead and wondered whether Sedgewick Bell would at this point care to see me. Certainly I represented some sort of truth to him about himself, yet at the same time I also seemed to have become a part of the very delusion that he had foisted on those around him. How far my boys would always stride upon the world's stage, yet how dearly I would always hope to change them! The bus arrived early, and I went inside the union hall to wait.

Shortly before noon the miners began to come in. I don't

know what I had expected, but I was surprised to see them looking as though they had indeed just come out of the mines. They wore hard hats, their faces were stained with dust, and their gloves and tool belts hung at their waists. For some reason, I had worn my St. Benedict's blazer, which I now removed. Reporters began to filter in as well, and by the time the noon whistle blew, the crowd was overflowing from the hall.

As the whistle subsided I heard the thump-thump of his helicopter, and through the door a moment later I saw the twisters of dust as it hovered into view from above. How clever was the man I had known as a boy! The craft had been repainted the colors of military camouflage, but he had left the sponsons the red, white, and blue of their previous incarnation. He jumped from the side door when the craft was still a foot above the ground, entered the hall at a jog, and was greeted with an explosion of applause. His aides lined the stairs to the high platform on which the microphone stood under a banner and a flag, and as he crossed the crowd toward them the miners jostled to be near him, knocking their knuckles against his hard hat, reaching for his hands and his shoulders, cheering like Romans at a chariot race.

I do not need to report on his eloquence, for I have dwelled enough upon it. When he reached the staircase and ascended to the podium, stopping first at the landing to wave and then at the top to salute the flag above him, jubilation swept among the throng. I knew then that he had succeeded in his efforts, that these miners counted him somehow as their own, so that when he actually spoke and they interrupted him with cheers, it was no more unexpected than the promises he made then to carry their interests with him to the Senate. He was masterful. I found my own arm upraised.

Certainly there were five hundred men in that hall, but there was only one with a St. Benedict's blazer over his shoulder and no hard hat on his head, so of course I should not have been surprised when within a few minutes one of his aides appeared beside me and told me that the candidate had asked for me at the podium. At that moment I saw Sedgewick Bell's glance pause for a moment on my face. There was a flicker of a smile on his lips, but then he looked away.

Is there no battle other than the personal one? Was Sedgewick Bell at that point willing to risk the future of his political ideas for whatever childhood demon I still remained to him? The next time he turned toward me, he gestured down at the floor, and in a moment the aide had pulled my arm and was escorting me toward the platform. The crowd opened as we passed, and the miners in their ignorance and jubilation were reaching to shake my hand. This was indeed a heady feeling. I climbed the steps and stood beside Sedgewick Bell at the smaller microphone. How it was to stand above the mass of men like that! He raised his hand and they cheered; he lowered it and they fell silent.

"There is a man here today who has been immeasurably important in my life," he whispered into his microphone.

There was applause, and a few of the men whistled. "Thank you," I said into my own. I could see the blue underbrims of five hundred hard hats turned up toward me. My heart was nearly bursting.

"My history teacher," he said, as the crowd began to cheer again. Flashbulbs popped and I moved instinctively toward the front of the platform. "Mr. Hundert," he boomed, "from forty-five years ago at Richmond Central High School."

It took me a moment to realize what he had said. By then he too was clapping and at the same time lowering his head in what must have appeared to the men below to be respect for me. The blood engorged my veins. "Just a minute," I said, stepping back to my own microphone. "I taught you at St. Benedict's School in Woodmere, Virginia. Here is the blazer."

Of course, it makes no difference in the course of history that as I tried to hold up the coat Sedgewick Bell moved swiftly across the podium, took it from my grip, and raised my arm high in his own, and that this pose, of all things, sent the miners into jubilation; it makes no difference that by the time I spoke, he had gestured with his hand so that one of his aides had already shut off my microphone. For one does not alter history without conviction. It is enough to know that I *did* speak, and certainly a consolation that Sedgewick Bell realized, finally, that I would.

He won that election not in small part because he managed to convince those miners that he was one of them. They were ignorant people, and I cannot blame them for taking to the shrewdly populist rhetoric of the man. I saved the picture that appeared the following morning in the *Gazette:* Senator Bell radiating all the populist magnetism of his father, holding high the arm of an old man who has on his face the remnants of a proud and foolish smile.

I still live in Woodmere, and I have found a route that I take now and then to the single high hill from which I can see the St. Benedict's steeple across the Passamic. I take two walks every day and have grown used to this life. I have even come to like it. I am reading of the ancient Japanese civilizations now, which I had somehow neglected before, and every so often one of my boys visits me.

One afternoon recently Deepak Mehta did so, and we shared

some brandy. This was in the fall of last year. He was still the quiet boy he had always been, and not long after he had taken a seat on my couch, I had to turn on the television to ease for him the burden of conversation. As it happened, the Senate Judiciary Committee was holding its famous hearings then, and the two of us sat there watching, nodding our heads or chuckling whenever the camera showed Sedgewick Bell sitting alongside the chairman. I had poured the brandy liberally, and whenever Sedgewick Bell leaned into the microphone and asked a question of the witness, Deepak would mimic his affected southern drawl. Naturally, I could not exactly encourage this behavior, but I did nothing to stop it. When he finished his drink I poured him another. This, of course, is perhaps the greatest pleasure of a teacher's life, to have a drink one day with a man he has known as a boy.

Nonetheless, I only wish we could have talked more than we actually did. But I am afraid that there must always be a reticence between a teacher and his student. Deepak had had another small heart attack, he told me, but I felt it would have been improper of me to inquire more. I tried to bring myself to broach the subject of Sedgewick Bell's history, but here again I was aware that a teacher does not discuss one boy with another. Certainly Deepak must have known about Sedgewick Bell as well, but probably because of his own set of St. Benedict's morals he did not bring it up with me. We watched Sedgewick Bell question the witness and then whisper into the ear of the chairman. Neither of us was surprised at his ascendence, I believe, because both of us were students of history. Yet we did not discuss this either. Still, I wanted desperately for him to ask me something more, and perhaps this was why I kept refilling his glass. I wanted him to ask, "How is it to be alone, sir, at this age?" or perhaps to say, "You have made a difference in my life, Mr. Hundert." But of course these were not things Deepak Mehta would ever say. A man's character is his character. Nonetheless, it was startling, every now and then when I looked over at the sunlight falling across his bowed head, to see that Deepak Mehta, the quietest of my boys, was now an old man.